A Shop's Fables

To Lynn —
my lovely,
amazing friend.
Judy

by

Judith Crowell

Illustrations by Bob Fanter

*for anyone who has ever
dreamed of, planned, obsessed over,
financed, participated in,
thrown, fainted at, attended, or run away
from a wedding.*

ISBN: 1-4196-9145-7
ISBN-13: 9781419691454

Available for purchase at: www.judithcrowell.com,
www.Amazon.com, www.Abebooks.com, www.Alibis.com

Visit at www.judithcrowell.com

Visit www.booksurge.com to order additional copies.

To

*the thousands of customers who passed through
our doors...*

*the jolly ninety-six percent
and
the not-so-jolly four percent
who added spice to our days
gray hairs to our heads
and
inspired both this book and my retirement.*

Thanks for the memories.

A SHOP'S FABLES

Table Of Contents

Table of Contents

.

Introduction

I had a shop in Missouri, at the foot of the Ladue hills.

It was a little shop catering to what, in a kinder, gentler time, would have been called the "carriage trade."

There were dresses for every special occasion in a woman's life. From flower girls to mothers-of-the-bride and groom—the most, shall we say, "challenging" category.

MOBs and MOGs (mothers-of-the-bride and mothers-of-the-groom) came through our doors expecting us to make them look twenty years younger, twenty pounds thinner and, occasionally, twenty percent more glamorous than their twenty-something replacements. All this within the constraints of:

- not outdoing the bride,
- not shattering the already badly battered wallet of the FOB (father-of-the-bride),
- not clashing with the colors of the bridesmaids, the other mother, the groom's ruffled shirt (pray to God, not!), the floral arrangements, the carpeting of the church, the stained glass windows, the wallpaper at the reception, the groom's eyes, the interior of the limo or the aura of the seasons (this for California weddings only).

Much easier for the MOGs (mothers-of-the-groom), who had already been told to wear beige and keep their mouths shut.

Brides had expectations going back to taking their

first steps of balancing precariously on three-inch silver sandals, swathed in yards of tulle and clutching a handful of garden posies in their trembling little hands.

Bridesmaids simply prayed for a dress that wasn't flammable, wouldn't end up posted on the Internet Worst Bridesmaid Dress List, didn't expose too much upper pulchritude or exceed their credit card limit.

Debutantes, still under mother's benevolent wing, wanted all the bells and whistles, lots of exposure of their upper pulchritude and were, for the most part, oblivious to credit card limits.

High school graduates, many required to wear long white dresses for graduation, just wanted out of high school.

And teenagers anticipating prom—ah, that is another story. Every seventeen-year-old knows that the *perfect* dress will make you irresistible to that tall, dark, handsome hunk you've been salivating over since seventh grade. And, like the virginal Sandy of *Grease* fame, will transform you into the end-of-the-movie, sleek-and-sexy Sandy version. All simply by finding the *perfect* dress.

Bat mitzvah girls always wanted to look ten years older, and flower girls just wanted to be able to twirl.

Based on this hormone-driven expectancy, I seriously considered calling this little yarn "Great Expectations," but that's already been done quite well.

Tucked away near a grove of crabapple trees, secluded from the main road and framed by four white columns and two pine trees, the shop evoked memories of a 1920s speak-easy.

A "Cheers" kind of place. You know…"Sometimes you want to go where everybody knows your name, and they're always glad you came." One of those kinds of places.

I suppose I was Sam, the bridal boutique bartender, serving up endless concoctions of gowns, listening to unrealistic expectations, and befriending every Carla, Rebecca, Lilith and occasional Norm who would come through our glass paneled French doors.

Their hopes and dreams were palpable, and I loved being part of their excitement. Occasionally, wedding plans and color schemes would become so all consuming and stressful that the reason for all their shopping and fa-la-la would be lost. Then boutique bartender Sam would offer up a bit of pragmatic philosophy along with her satin and lace concoctions.

Looking to create the perfect wedding?
- No such thing.
- The wedding won't be perfect.
- Something will go wrong. *No one will notice.*

Looking to create the perfect marriage?
- No such thing.
- The marriage won't be perfect.
- Lots of things will go wrong.
- Notice them.
- Love can fix them.

Searching for the fountain of youth in a dress?

A panacea for loneliness in a necklace?

A guarantee for a date to the prom from a four-hundred-dollar gown?

• No such thing.

What I did do, and loved doing for some twenty years, was to help every customer who walked out of our doors come as close as possible to living up to the wild expectations they had when they first walked in our doors—a dress to make them feel more beautiful than they ever had before on their day of days. No extra charge for philosophy.

Then one morning, after unlocking the front door for business, straightening up the glittering gowns lined up like so many empty princesses, vacuuming up the never-ending tiny crystal beads and white threads littering the dark green carpet and selecting some romantic Frank Sinatra ballads for the sound system, I glanced at the appointment book. Scheduled for ten o'clock was a favorite client, Molly Davenport. Only now she was Molly Davenport Morehouse. No longer was she buying a prom dress, a debutante ball gown, wedding gown or umpteenth bridesmaid dress for herself. She was looking for a prom dress for her daughter.

Then and there, I knew it was time to close up shop.

I knew I would miss playing a small part in so many special events. Knew I'd miss the customers, designers, friendships with my staff, and the buying trips to New York.

I'd been a widow (a word I despise) for four years,

had watched my daughter, son-in-law and grandchildren move to California, and longed for more time with them and my youngest daughter in town. I had held a lot of hands over the last twenty years and, who knew, maybe there was somebody out there waiting to hold mine.

So I sold out.

I sold to a mother/daughter team who continue to sell the loveliest gowns in town and have learned very quickly that ninety-six percent of the bridal business is jolly. It's the four percent that keeps you checking the mirror every morning for gray hairs. Or as a wise woman once said, "It just wouldn't be a picnic without the ants."

Now it's time to talk about the other four percent, the ants. And to paraphrase another wise woman, Teddy Roosevelt's infamous daughter Alice: "Why don't you pull up a chair, sit right here by me and let's talk."

A Bride's Maids

"Mrs. Crowell, I'm counting on you to help me," a frazzled young bride pleaded with me over the phone. "It's taken me almost a month to get everybody together to see my wedding gown and pick out my bridesmaid dresses. But we can all make it this Friday at three o'clock. Will that work for you?"

"Let me check my appointment book, Christine."

"Please, please, work me in. Four of my twelve bridesmaids are flying in for this appointment. My mother will be coming with a little gift for everyone, a darling beaded bracelet she made with my married initials and wedding date spelled out in beads for them to wear at the wedding, and my future mother-in-law is bringing her camera to film a video for the rehearsal dinner. Oh, and she might want to look at a dress for herself while we're there.

"My four flower girls are getting picked up early from school, and you need to know, one's going through a tremendous growth spurt, although I guess her mother could put her on a diet, and one doesn't want to be in the wedding. Her mother, my matron-of-honor, just had twin boys. Wait 'til you see them. They're adorable. She's bringing them because she doesn't feel comfortable leaving them with a sitter yet. Little Jonathan has projectile vomiting. I think the reluctant flower girl is just jealous of all the attention the twins are getting. I'm hoping by the time of the wedding, the twins will be able to walk down the aisle as my ring bearers. Do you carry any of those precious

Little Lord Fauntelroy white short panted suits for boys? Their mother is nursing and her boobs are humongous, but she'll probably stop nursing right before the wedding, so her bust will deflate and she'll need to be measured for her dress with that in mind.

"There is one thing I'm worried about. My very best friend since kindergarten wants to come along for this appointment, and I just can't say no to her because she's been so good to me through thick and thin. She won't be a bridesmaid because that would make the number of attendants thirteen, and she understands the trauma of that. Anyway, she weighs close to three hundred pounds, and we figured that bridesmaid dresses don't come in her size.

"I'm sure you'll be as tactful as always with this situation. Have you checked your schedule yet?"

Not only had I checked my appointment book and realized it was my thirty-eighth wedding anniversary and that we had dinner plans that night, but, listening to Christine, I'd had a near death experience. A vision flashed before my eyes—a vision of our pristine fifteen-by-eleven foot bridesmaids' showroom, all one hundred and sixty-five square feet at twenty-nine dollars per square foot, designed for a maximum of four customers and containing eight racks of sample dresses, a checkout desk, display mannequin, two delicate white wicker arm chairs, one white wicker end table, a glass jewelry display case, two floral decoupage lamps, a dressing room enclosure, wall-to-wall mirrors to create the illusion of space and reflect infinite images of women of every size and shape imaginable scrutinizing themselves in various bridesmaid dresses.

Jammed into this vision, in this intimate enclave of femininity, were twenty-five bodies:

- One crazed bride.
- Eight well-rested local bridesmaids armed with words of fashion advice.
- Four jetlagged bridesmaids lugging four carry on bags.
- One mother-of-the-bride with dollar signs floating in her corneas.
- One mother-of-the-groom directing a video.
- Three just-sprung-from-school, overly tired flower girls.
- One flower girl who didn't want to be a flower girl.
- Two infants in a four-by-four stroller, one inclined to projectile vomiting.
- One obese very best friend, a time bomb of frustration waiting to explode.
- Two of my most patient sales staff.
- And me.

Oh my God.

An appointment of one and a half hours was our standard procedure. No way was this cast of characters going to be finished by four-thirty—or five, or six, or seven, for that matter.

My husband had made dinner reservations at one

of our favorite restaurants to celebrate our anniversary. We would reminisce over champagne about our own wedding day, slow dance to the seductive tempo of our song, "Moonglow" (from the movie *Picnic*), and under a full moon, would drive home where he'd carry me over the threshold, tear off my clothes and make mad passionate love to me into the wee hours of the morning, just like on our wedding night thirty-eight years before.

Brides are not the only ones with fantasies.

"Yes, Christine. I've checked the schedule, and Friday at three will be fine."

"Oh, thank goodness. I was so afraid I'd have to start contacting everybody all over again."

"No need to do that, but there are a couple of things I want to mention to you. First, do you really want your friends to see your gown before the wedding day? It looks so beautiful on you and will make the most impact on them if you wait until right before you walk down the aisle. Your groom, of course, will see it for the first time as you proceed down the aisle—the ultimate impact."

"You're right, Mrs. Crowell, I hadn't really thought about it that way."

Round one—my corner.

"My other suggestion to you is based upon years of experience, and that is that the more people you have trying to make a decision on one dress, the more difficult it becomes. With so many different body types, budgets and opinions on style, you will be terribly frustrated and find it almost impossible to come to a decision.

"And you know how small our showroom is. I really think you'd be much better off to limit your appointment here to one or two bridesmaids. You've been a bridesmaid several times. Now it's your turn to select the dress you want them to wear."

"Oh, no, I couldn't do that. Besides, I made sure that all my maids are pretty, with the same perfect body types, and that they have enough money to meet the standards of my wedding. And, as far as differing opinions, we all have the same taste in clothes, and I know they all want me to have the bridesmaid dresses I like the best. We'll all be in agreement. I just know it."

Round two—bride's corner.

All right, Christine, then we'll look forward to seeing you at three o'clock on Friday."

Now, dear reader, you *must* know where this is headed. The outcome of this saga is almost too sad and predictable to tell.

But, I shall.

First to arrive on Friday at quarter to three was the MOG, wanting to check out lighting for the video. At ten to three, obese very best friend/time bomb arrived and headed straight for one of the delicate white wicker armchairs. MOB and bride, positively beaming, arrived together in time to greet all eleven bridesmaids, each clad in outfits ranging from low slung, bare midriff jeans and tank tops to two piece, navy blue, vice-president-of-a-bank suit attire. MOB proudly handed out her gifts of tulle wrapped, hand-made bracelet to each maid, with clear, forceful instructions that they were to be worn on the right wrist the day of the wedding.

So as not to be overly accessorized, Miss Bank Vice-President removed her one piece of jewelry, a single strand of pearls, and with profuse thank-yous placed the gleaming bride's soon to be married initials on her right wrist. Miss Low-Slung Jeans decided it made a much better anklet than a bracelet, but promised to conform at the wedding and wear it in the designated place. Remaining reactions were varied, with polite thank-yous, a few sidelong glances and a giggle or two. Three bracelets were left behind. One was found under a cushion. One turned up in the vacuum cleaner bag two weeks later. One never did see the light of day.

Absent bridesmaid number twelve had missed her flight and wouldn't show up until five-thirty. ADD-hyper is the only way to describe the three flower girls, ecstatic to be out of school half an hour early and the centers of such attention. Number four simply sulked.

Seating choices included the one remaining delicate white wicker arm chair, a couple of benches brought in for the occasion, the dark green carpet, the wicker end table and the checkout desk. As soon as everyone found their places, the matron-of-honor arrived with a stroller—a *big* stroller—and babies, who were strategically placed opposite the floor to ceiling mirror in an effort to keep them entertained and thwart anything projectile being hurled in the vicinity of the eight racks of sample dresses.

My saintly sales associates suggested that we begin by looking at flower girl dresses. Not a lot of choices here. The bride wanted them in white and unless flower girl number two spent the next few months with a brick on her head and a banana/water diet, there were only a few dresses that were going to work for this growing-as-we-speak nine year old. A perky, organza, twirlable white dress was chosen with relatively little fuss and measurements were taken for the willing three. Miss Sulk remained sprawled on the floor, making faces into the mirror, so a size was determined for her using pure guesswork. Chances were she wasn't going to wear it anyway.

Then it was time for the main event.

In my mind, looking back on it all, it always plays out as a one act French farce.

CURTAIN RISES
BRIDE ENTERS STAGE RIGHT, HAVING TAKEN A BREAK FOR A DRINK OF WATER AND A COUPLE OF VALIUMS.

BRIDE: Mrs. Crowell is going to show us

some of the best styles, then you can all start trying them on.

MRS. CROWELL: We've got all the latest styles, and you're welcome to look at everything, but, to make it easier for you, I'd like to suggest some of our most flattering dresses. We have nine different designers, about fifteen styles per designer and each style comes in several different colors. Bridesmaids love our two-pieces because they can be mixed and matched lots of different ways. So, with all these choices, I've tried to help by narrowing our selection down to some of our bestsellers. We have two dressing rooms, one large and one small, so if you don't mind sharing the large room, everyone can take turns trying on dresses and then we'll eliminate as we go. Then when a choice is made, we can get everyone measured for her dress.

THESE ARE THE LAST COHERENT WORDS SPOKEN BY MRS. CROWELL.

MATRON-OF-HONOR: Before we start, let me spread this plastic tarp on the rug. The babies nursed right before we came, and when Jonathan wakes up, his little tummy may be upset. I'll just lay it right over Isabelle's Cheerios that she spilled on the rug. That eighteen-month-old stage is so precious, although clumsy. She's going to look like an angel in her white dress.

FLOWER GIRL #3 (KATE): What about me? Everyone's always saying how cute Isabelle is. She's a pain.

BRIDESMAID #5: Kate, shame on you. I keep telling you...you're as adorable as Isabelle. Now quit fooling with those drop earrings. Maybe Mrs. Crowell will let you rearrange the jewelry case later. I brought you and your sister plenty of books and magic markers to play with. Let's help spread this tarp out. Oops, it looks like it didn't get washed since the last time it was used.

BRIDE CROSSING CAREFULLY OVER TARP TO DISPLAY RACK OF DRESSES.

BRIDESMAID #3: Vera is so over with. Everybody does Vera Wang and I'm sick of it.

BRIDESMAID #7: I agree, and her fabrics wrinkle all the time. Especially the satin.

BRIDESMAID #4: That's baloney. She's great, for destination weddings especially.

Barefoot, beachside, like all my friends in California are doing.

MOB: This wedding is at St. Elizabeth's Church in Clayton.

BRIDESMAID #1: Look at this great strapless.

BRIDESMAID #6: I can't wear strapless. My boobs won't hold it up and it just makes my hips look bigger than they already are.

BRIDESMAID #1: Strapless is great.

BRIDESMAID #6: I can't wear strapless.

BRIDE: I like strapless.

MOB: St. Elizabeth's doesn't allow strapless.

SALES ASSOCIATE ENTERS UP-STAGE, STEPPING CAREFULLY OVER CHEERIOS AND TARP.

SAINTLY SALES ASSOCIATE #1: Here are four of our best styles from Currie Bonner, one of our newest—

MISS LOW-SLUNG JEANS: Much too conservative.

MISS BANK VICE-PRESIDENT: I don't think so. They're simple and elegant and with a strand of pearls, and, of course, our lovely new initial bracelets, they'd be perfect.

MISS LOW-SLUNG JEANS: Boring, boring—like most of your wardrobe.

FIVE BRIDESMAIDS CROSS TO JOIN BRIDE DOWN-STAGE RIGHT TO DISPLAY RACK, EACH PULLING TWO TO THREE DRESSES.

SAINTLY SALES ASSOCIATE #1: Look at their color chart. So many beautiful colors. That's okay, Gretl, we'll get that lollipop unstuck from the chart for you. Don't cry. Maybe Mommy will give you some of Isabelle's Cheerios that haven't fallen on the rug yet. That's a girl. And yes, you're so smart— that pink sample is much prettier with some of the raspberry lollipop stuck to it.

BRIDESMAIDS DOWN-STAGE RIGHT CROSS BACK TO DOWN STAGE LEFT, BRINGING DRESSES. DRESSES ARE BEING HUNG OVER CHAIRS, HANDLE OF STROLLER, MOB'S LAP, DRESSING ROOM SWINGING DOORS, CHECK OUT DESK, MANNEQUIN, CHANDELIER AND JONATHAN.

BRIDESMAID #4: Does that price tag say $265? That's ridiculous. The last wedding I was in I paid only $175.

BRIDESMAID #1: And the dresses looked it. You could see right through the skirt when you walked down the aisle. Didn't you know that?

BRIDESMAID #4: Good grief, no. Why would you tell me that now?

BRIDESMAID #1: The sage green drained all the color out of your face, too.

Might as well tell you the whole truth.

BRIDE: I'm not considering sage green. My color is pink.

BRIDESMAID #10: Oh, my God. Pink? With my red hair?

BRIDE: It'll be stunning.

MOB: I've already decided on deep rose for myself.

MOG: Guess that means I can do red. It's my very best color. Oh, this is so much fun—and I'm getting all these wonderful reactions on video. Yes, dear, that looks like a delicious lollipop, but try to keep your sticky little fingers off the camera lens and satin dresses.

MATRON-OF-HONOR: Are we going to start trying on soon, Christine? Jonathan's been so good, I think I'll top him off with a little more milk. You don't mind, do you? It's just us girls.

> *FLOWER GIRL #2 (GRETL) CEASES MAKING FACES AT KATE AND ISABELLE IN MIRRORS.*

FLOWER GIRL #2 (GRETL): That's gross.

MATRON-OF-HONOR: It's Mother Nature's way, darling. Someday you'll be a mommy, too, and want to cuddle and love and feed your baby.

FLOWER GIRL #2 (GRETL): No way. I'm never getting married, and I'll never have a baby stuck to me like that. It's gross.

> *MISS SULK RISES FROM CHEERIO LITTERED RUG TO GLARE AT GRETL.*

MISS SULK: Then you'd better not be a flower girl and wear that stupid white dress. It's just like getting married.

FLOWER GIRL #2 (GRETL): Is not.

MISS SULK: Is too.

FLOWER GIRL #2 (GRETL): Is not. You're only in kindergarten. You don't know anything.

MOB: Out of the mouths of babes— such little darlings.

> *MATRON-OF-HONOR GRABS MISS SULK BY THE ARM, BALANCING BABY JONATHAN, WHO IS BEGINNING TO HICCUP, IN HER OTHER ARM AND RAPIDLY EXITS RIGHT WING.*

MATRON-OF-HONOR: I'll be right back.

MOG: No hurry.

> *BRIDE EXITS STAGE RIGHT FOR MORE VALIUM.*

SAINTLY SALES ASSOCIATE #1: Here, let me pick up a few of these skirts and tops or we'll forget what combinations you've put together. These strapless tops will have to go.

BRIDESMAID #6: Let's hear it for St. Elizabeth.

BRIDE, MATRON-OF-HONOR, MISS SULK AND JONATHAN, FRESHLY DIAPERED, RE-ENTER STAGE RIGHT.

BRIDE TO BRIDESMAID #5: Why don't you start first since your bust is smaller and your hips bigger. If it looks good on you, it'll look good on everyone.

BRIDESMAID #1: I'll share the larger dressing room with someone. Just keep the clothes coming, so we can get this over with.

BRIDE TO OBESE VERY BEST FRIEND/TIME BOMB: You've been so quiet. Are you feeling okay? Or are you just being your usual sweet, helpful self? I've been trying to think of a title to give you. How about Very Best Friend In Charge Of Zippers? Wouldn't that be fun?

OBESE VERY BEST FRIEND/TIME BOMB: Sure.

BRIDESMAID #1: This one's not so bad, if you get rid of the big bow on the butt.

BRIDESMAID #7: It's too expensive and it wrinkles.

BRIDESMAID #4: In California, nobody worries about wrinkles.

MOB: This isn't California.

BRIDESMAID #1: How about this one? Great neckline, and I love the deep turquoise.

BRIDE: My color is pink.

SAINTLY SALES ASSOCIATE #2: Let's give the next group a turn. I think you three like all six of these dresses, so let's concentrate on them and eliminate the other four.

BRIDESMAID #3: That's not fair, I liked one of those other ones.

BRIDESMAID #7: Come on, it's almost five o'clock already, and I've got a date at six. I don't like any of them, but you don't hear me complaining.

BRIDESMAID #3: I'm not complaining. We all agreed to try to get along for Christine's sake, and I'm trying my best. I'm the one who's bloated with her period. I shouldn't even be trying clothes on today.

BRIDESMAID #11: Give me a break. You're always bloated.

MATRON-OF-HONOR: I'm the one who should be complaining. But I'm not. How'd you like to be trying on bridesmaid dresses with thirty pounds of extra baby fat and a triple D bustline constantly leaking? If I wasn't trying to convince you-know-who how much fun it's going to be to be a flower girl, I'd have stayed home with the twins. No way am I getting measured today.

BRIDESMAID #3: Me either.

BRIDESMAID #4: Or me. I had a cheeseburger, French fries and a bowl of chili for lunch.

BRIDESMAID #11: Oh, my God. Look at this one. The V-neckline plunges down to my navel.

SAINTLY SALES ASSOCIATE #2: You have it on backwards.

MISS LOW-SLUNG JEANS: I like the Vera Wang halter with straight, slit skirt the best.

MISS BANK VICE-PRESIDENT: Too sexy.

BRIDESMAID #7: You need to lighten up.

MISS BANK VICE-PRESIDENT: Lighten up? Or start dressing like a hooker? Like some people I know.

MOB: Now girls.

BRIDESMAID #11: My vote is for the scoop neck, A-line dress by Siri.

BRIDESMAID #5: It did hide my hips.

BRIDESMAID #7: I hated it.

BRIDESMAID #3: Maybe in a darker color, like navy or brown. Oh, that's right, we have to wear pink.

BRIDESMAID #10: I can't stand pink.

BRIDESMAID #1: I wore pink in the last wedding I was in and the photos were all so washed out that we looked like we were nude.

OBESE VERY BEST FRIEND/TIME BOMB: I like pink.

BRIDE, WITH DEER IN THE HEADLIGHTS EXPRESSION, STAGGERS TO CENTER-STAGE FRONT, HOLDS HER HEAD HIGH, MUSTERING UP AS MUCH REMAINING DIGNITY AS SHE CAN.

BRIDE: Mrs. Crowell, it's six-thirty and everyone must be getting tired and hungry, so I think I'll give you a call next week to discuss this.

BRIDE EXITS UP-STAGE IN GREAT HASTE. MOB FOLLOWS CLOSELY BEHIND.
CURTAIN LOWERS

That, dear reader, is how I choose to remember that day. It was worse—much worse.

Christine did call the next week, coming in alone one week later to select a pink A-line, dupioni silk dress by Siri at $285.

Her out-of-town bridesmaids called in their measurements. Local bridesmaids came back in to be measured, filtering in over the next two months according to their various whims and monthly cycles. Individually, they were very nice young women.

Hoping to shed as many ounces of baby fat as possible, the maid-of-honor was the last to be measured, bearing the good news that Miss Sulk was warming up to the idea of being a flower girl and that Jonathan's tummy troubles were history.

As for our thirty-eighth anniversary: We never did make it to our favorite restaurant. Never reminisced over champagne, or slow danced to "Moonglow." The moon wasn't full, and my husband didn't (couldn't) carry me over the threshold or tear off my clothes. However, all was not lost, and, fortunately, I had no appointments scheduled for the following morning.

Brides are not the only ones making love.

"True friends stab you in the front."

Oscar Wilde

The Lotus Girl

A lovely lotus blossom floated into the store one rain charged April afternoon. She had long, flowing, coal black hair, skin the color of ripe honey, and the mysteries of the Orient buried deep in her eyes. Her diminutive height would not have reached the fifty-five inch mark, if ours had been the kind of store with a height chart posted on the exit door to facilitate in identifying and apprehending fleeing thieves.

Her voice was lilting and soft and sweetly accented and made me want to run to the phone and book an immediate flight to China. With her was a tall, blonde, blue-eyed, Midwestern couple—prime candidates for prom king and queen.

And it was prom season, only our second since opening the store. Not yet had the prom dress scene deteriorated into no-win fiasco status for us.

Perched one story above in my balcony office, I could hear my daughter, who worked with me part-time, greet them.

"Hi, I'm Kim. I'll bet you're here looking for prom dresses, and I see that you have wisely brought along a male opinion."

"That's right. I'm Lien. This is Alicia, and we're both looking for dresses. The one in the window caught our eye and Curt's. This is my friend, Curt."

"Hi, Curt. That dress is one of my favorites, too, and would look great on either one of you girls," said my daughter. "Let's go back and find some more.

Here's a chair for you, Curt. Just sit back, enjoy and critique."

I continued to watch from above as the girls emerged again and again from the dressing rooms. Giggling, laughing, kidding each other, and reveling in the joy of being seventeen and healthy and pretty and friends.

"Oh, Alicia, that blue satin's beautiful on you. Makes your eyes look even bluer. I think I like it better than the short green one."

"Thanks, Lien, and I love that deep purple on you, but you look great in everything you try on. Agreed, Curt?"

"Agreed. Wait 'til Gary sees you in that one. Is it your favorite?"

"I'm not sure. I probably should wait until my mother gets here. She said she wanted to see the dresses."

"We can try a few more. Your mother might be delayed by the rain," said Kim. "Are you all seniors?"

"We are," said Curt. "Lien came in last year as a junior, but she made friends so fast that it seems like she's been with us since freshman year."

"It really does, doesn't it?" replied Lien, emerging once again in a strapless ruby red long gown, clutching the extra five or six inches up off the floor to keep from tripping. "Everyone's been so good to me, especially you and Alicia. It's hard to come in as a junior. I don't know what I'd have done without you guys."

The rain charged air had turned into a sudden spring hailstorm, muffling the shop's stereo system and conversation below me. A few more outfits were paraded in front of Curt, when I noticed a car pull up in the front parking lot, a woman and umbrella dash through the hail and heard Lien say that her mother had arrived.

"Great," said Kim. "Wait 'til she sees how fabulous you look in these dresses."

As the hail continued to pummel the roof overhead, I picked up snatches of subdued conversation, dressing room doors quietly opening and closing and saw Curt move to the front room where he began to pace, no longer offering opinions. As hail will do, it ended as abruptly as it had begun, and with the ending came a tense quiet, both outside and inside. Something was very wrong.

Kim came up the winding staircase to my office. "Mother, you need to come downstairs."

Curt was standing at the front door, his eyes locked in horror with Alicia's frightened blue eyes. Alicia, in the blue satin gown she would eventually wear to prom, was leaning against the dressing room door, tears welling in her eyes.

Hidden beneath the largest circular rack of dresses and curled up in a fetal position, was tiny Lien, hands covering her face in shame, as her mother spewed forth a torrent of insults, Chinese abuses and invectives, mercifully for us, understood only by Lien. Occasionally in her tirade, some English words would break through. Words like tramp, who, do, you, think, you, are, ungrateful, cheap, whore. Each punctuated by a stab of her umbrella.

Appalled, I approached her, asked Kim to see to Lien, and led the ranting mother into the front entry room.

"We cannot have this in our shop. I'll have to ask you to leave. Now."

"She will not buy a dress here. I will not allow it. She will not wear anything showing skin. I will not allow it."

"Please, you must leave. Right now."

"Lien's coming with me."

"No, she's not. She came with her friends, and we'll see to it that she is safe and that she leaves with her friends. Leave."

I was shaking as I watched this woman drive away. Kim and Alicia had helped Lien up from the floor and were wiping the tears from her face, when Curt turned to me and said, "This is nothing new. It's been reported. Lien lives with this most of the time. Everyone in our class watches out for her and tries to spend as much time as possible with her so she's not at home very much. She's an amazing student with an A average and a scholaship to Duke, so she'll be leaving home soon and says she'll never come back."

"But in the meantime, can you really protect her?"

"We're doing our damnedest. We'll come back in a few days. We're all pitching in to buy her a prom-dress. She's going with my best friend, Gary. He's crazy about her."

"We'll help out with the cost of the dress. Just stay here for a little while. I'll shut the door so no one else comes in. Are you sure you should take her home?"

"We'll stay out for a while, grab a burger and give her mother time to cool down. Thanks for all your help."

My help? I did nothing, really, looking back on it. It haunted me to think of this fragile child and her staunch protectors, trying their best, in the only way they knew how, to keep their friend from harm.

I learned afterwards that the name Lien signifies lotus. The essence of the lotus flower is often used to help abused animals survive and eventually forget their oppression and abuse. The flower itself emerges from impure water to blossom into a pure, uncontaminated flower. A symbol of purity and rebirth.

I think often of her, the lovely Lotus girl, and I pray that, like her namesake, she, too, has been reborn, finding safety and love.

"Help thy brother's boat across, and lo!
thine own has reached the shore."

Hindu proverb

The Pouf Dress

*I*n the early 1990s, before heading east to 7ᵗʰ Avenue, I was still buying at the Dallas Market Center (DMC), the world's largest wholesale merchandise mart with one hundred acres, over five million square feet of showrooms, all under one roof. Cracker crumbs for remembering one's way recommended.

One afternoon, after misplacing my cracker crumbs and enjoying a lunch of chicken enchiladas and a Texas-sized, salted, on-the-rocks margarita, I stumbled into an unknown showroom—one I'd never noticed before. I had no appointment. Nor did I have any OTB (Open To Buy) for the bordello look being featured, but I found myself spellbound by rack after rack of shiny, feathered, flounced, fringed, sequined dresses. Who in the name of heaven wore these things? Dallas Cowboy Cheerleaders, I presumed, as several young women with blinding blonde bouffant hair and Barbie doll bodies began modeling these creations.

The sales rep, Bob—why are so many sales reps named Bob?—a moonlighting used-car salesman with a slippery, wavy, shinola black hairpiece, was straining to be heard over the rock music blaring out of the showroom's sound system.

"At a bargain price of seventy-five bucks, this little number is called Lustrous. It's available in sizes 2 to 42 and in all thirty-six colors you see here on the color chart. Mark this little number up two hundred and fifty percent and you've got a winner, folks. Here comes Breathless, Blissful and Seduction. No question on these, folks. You gotta' have 'em."

As this fashion show nightmare proceeded, I spied a short taffeta dress smashed in between a rack of loose-virtue dresses. This one could have been called Tasteful. In fact, I wasn't even sure it belonged in Bob's showroom.

It was strapless, with a tightly sheered bodice all the way down to mid-hip, where it flounced out in poufs all the way around to the above-knee hem. It would streamline where it needed to streamline, conceal where it needed to conceal. And had just enough pizzazz and sexiness to placate both mother and daughter. Not an easy task.

Wholesale price was $95 and with a Keystone mark-up (the industry standard one hundred percent), plus an additional twenty percent mark up for navigating the DMC without getting lost and to cover the cost of my Texas-sized margarita, I figured I had a dilly of a prom dress for spring delivery at a mere $230 retail price. In thirty-six colors, no less.

I ordered two dozen in various sizes and colors for March delivery.

They arrived so tightly packed in their enormous cardboard box, that, with the first puncture of our razor box cutter, the box literally exploded, sending pink, turquoise and teal taffeta poufs flying all over the stock room. At $230, you not only were going to get your money's worth out of these bombshells, you were buying a dress that was indestructible.

The pouf skirt was so structured that the dresses didn't need a hanger. We displayed them by standing them up in a rainbowed row, like little gender-confused soldiers.

Then, they did what they were supposed to do. Like proverbial hotcakes, they flew out of the store. I re-ordered and re-ordered, until I was sure that every prom in town would have at least one of these pouf dresses in attendance. One prom ended up with six and not one duplication in color.

A local paper ran a photo of all six girls lined up in a can-can pose, delighted with their pouf prom uniforms and proving that sometimes six women can show up at the same event and wearing the same dress and not have it end in bloodshed. And that occasionally, a bit of the bordello look can be a good thing.

"Remember that always dressing in understated good taste is the same as playing dead."

Anonymous

Mrs. Dorsett And Mrs. Blanton

*H*ardly a week went by without a customer coming in and asking for the same dress she'd seen on a bride or a mother or a bridesmaid at a wedding a week or so before.

Raven haired, flat chested, pear bottomed Julia wanted blonde, voluptuous, no hipped Renata's sweetheart neckline, strapless, side-slit, sheath wedding gown.

Mrs. Carmichel, with a firm budget of $395, wanted Mrs. Rockefeller's $2,000 designer gown. And five-year-old Allison wanted to wear the exact same dress her sister Lucy had worn when she was a flower girl in her Aunt Jane's wedding, but refused—stomp, stomp, stomp of her little foot—to wear the hand-me-down version.

This copycat mentality was contrary to everything we tried to do. We had never drafted a mission statement. Life's too short for that. But we all knew what our mission was: To treat each customer as an individual and help her find her own most flattering look.

We used to laugh about one of the earliest Vera Wang designs for bridesmaids. It was a scoop neck, sleeveless tank top paired with a side pleated, A-line skirt, and it gave everyone a body like Cameron Diaz. Well, almost everyone. It came in a fabric called *faille* (pronounced "file"), a miraculous blend of cotton and polyester, ribbed in teeny, tiny vertical lines. Think baby corduroy. Creating a structured, cinched-in top, an hourglass waist and an A-line, tee-pee bottom. In various colors, it paraded down the aisles of every saint's church, synagogue and flower-lined garden path in St. Louis. Short or tall, narrow or wide, it made our bridesmaids happy and paid many a month's rent.

Our mission of individuality was sorely tested the day Mrs. Dorsett walked in the shop.

She didn't want to be shown anything, didn't want to try anything on and didn't want to hear about prices. She wanted to order the exact same dress that Mrs. Blanton had worn two weeks prior. And she needed a rush order since her own daughter's wedding was only two months away.

I tried my best to dissuade her from that particular dress, knowing that Mrs. Blanton wouldn't be thrilled and that it wouldn't be the best style for Mrs. Dorsett.

We had an array of platitudes handy for occasions such as this and, depending on the situation, would toss out phrases such as, "Be your own best self," "Imitation is the sincerest form of flattery" (that one for Mrs. Blanton when she found out that Mrs. Dorsett was wearing her dress), and one very ill-advised time when I was totally harassed and uttered, "Monkey see, monkey do."

No platitudes were working for Mrs. Dorsett. She wanted Mrs. Blanton's dress. Period.

I took her fifty percent deposit—store policy on all special orders—and five weeks later the dress arrived.

Mrs. Dorsett came in immediately, saw the dress on the hanger and was ecstatic.

Mrs. Dorsett went into the dressing room, tried on the dress, which fit perfectly, came out of the dressing room and announced, "I'm not buying this dress. It's not the same dress that Mrs. Blanton wore."

"Oh, yes, Mrs. Dorsett, it is, and it fits you perfectly."

Now, dear reader, I hadn't been a Girl Scout for naught and was prepared with a photo, which Mrs. Blanton's daughter had brought in the week before.

There, in glorious color, standing with the bride in the receiving line, was the five foot, nine inches, bust thirty-eight, waist twenty-seven, hips thirty-eight, forty-seven year old, Jane Seymour look-alike MOB. In the exact same dress being currently worn by the five foot, two inches, bust forty-two, waist thirty-seven, hips forty-three, sixty-three year old, Ugly Betty look-alike MOB.

"This is not the dress I wanted. I wanted to look like Mrs. Blanton in the photo. It does not look the same. I demand my money back."

Words failed me.

The old maxim of knowing when to cut your losses rescued me. I said, "I'm sorry, Mrs. Dorsett, that you're unhappy with your dress. We want everyone to be happy with the way they look on their special day. I'll credit your Visa right away."

To this day, I have no idea what Mrs. Dorsett ended up wearing. Hopefully, she went home, had a stiff drink followed by a much needed reality check, and then found something lovely already hanging in her closet.

"Why should we all dress after the same fashion? The frost never paints my windows twice alike."

Lydia Maria Child

A Teal Satin Gown

ꝒＫ *S*peaking of reality checks, I'm reminded of a blustery, snowy afternoon when my daughter was working with me. Perched in my upstairs balcony office, I heard the front door open and saw Kim greet the tall, attractive woman entering the store.

Kim, kind reader, could sell bikinis to Eskimos, a strapless gown to a Franciscan nun or the shirt off her mother's back. Never turn down an order, was her motto.

- Don't like those buttons? No problem, we'll change them.
- Want pierced earrings instead of clip? We'll fix them.
- Need it in three weeks? No problem.
- Would love to have it in a week? Sure thing.
- Want to wear it tonight? You're in luck. My mother just happens to be your size and has that same blouse hanging at home in her closet. I'll run out and get it for you, so you can wear it tonight.

I'm not kidding. That last one really happened.

So, I was not prepared for the following exchange, which took place on that cold, December afternoon.

"Hi, how are you? I'm Kim. How can I help you?"

"I'm looking for a satin gown for a black tie event. It must match this teal swatch and have a black velvet bolero top with long sleeves. I want it to have a straight skirt, drop waist and square neckline. I need a size 16 with extra length, and it has to have a side zipper because I can't reach a back zipper. And I need it by next weekend."

Reality check on the way.

"Well, that sounds like it would be a very nice gown. Unfortunately, I don't have it. Nor do I think any of the other shops along here would. I think the only place you may find it is on Cloud Nine."

Yes, gentle reader, that's what my darling daughter said.

Even more shocking was the customer's reply.

"Will you please give me the directions to get there?"

I honestly thought I was hearing things and glared at my daughter as she staggered, half laughing, half crying up our wrought iron, circular stairway.

"Are you out of your mind?" I asked. "Was that some kind of dumb blonde joke, or what?"

"Sorry, Mother. I couldn't help it. One of those PMS days, I guess. Think I'll go home."

"Where's the man could ease a heart like a satin gown?"

Dorothy Parker

Miss Alice Blue Gown

A pageant contestant and her mother walked in one day. I was alone in the store, which turned out to be a good thing, since I couldn't have handled this encounter with anyone else around. Especially my daughters.

Her title, she announced, was Miss Hog Hollow County, and she was competing in the upcoming Miss Missouri competition. She was running on a platform of eliminating poverty for unwed mothers in her hometown and was in the store to purchase five outfits (the sixth, a lime-green bikini, had been purchased elsewhere, thank God). She needed a traveling dress, an interview dress, a photo session dress, a long gown for the formal wear competition, and, most important of all, another long gown for the talent part of the competition.

Ka-chink, ka-chink was my immediate reaction, as I mentally tallied up what promised to be a very nice sale from this poverty fighting beauty contestant. It also occurred to me that perhaps a check for $5,000 made payable to the Hog Hollow Unwed Mothers Association would have been a much more direct and efficient way of helping out.

I kept these thoughts to myself.

Her mother said that it was very important for the final gown to be blue, Alice blue, since her daughter's talent was singing, and her song was "Sweet Little Alice Blue Gown."

"I hope I can find the right shade of blue, Mrs. Crowell. It has to match my eyes exactly, which, as you can see, are a perfect sky blue."

She said this as she leaned into me, ten inches or so away from my face, across the checkout desk. Eyeball to eyeball, so I could really check out those pageant blue eyes and find just the right color for her.

"Everybody tells me I've picked the perfect song to sing. Would you like to hear it?"

And without waiting for an answer, at that point twenty-four inches away from me, still across the checkout desk, with a beaming mother watching my every move and expression, she began to sing— singing the song she was counting on to catapult her from Miss Hog Hollow to Miss Missouri to Miss USA all the way to Miss Universe.

> In my sweet little Alice blue gown,
> When I first wandered down into town,
> I was both proud and shy,
> As I felt every eye,
> And in every shop window, I primped, passing by.
> A new manner of fashion I'd found,
> And the world seemed to smile all around.
> 'Til it wilted, I wore it,
> I'll always adore it,
> My sweet little Alice blue gown.

I regret, patient reader, having to put you through all that, but that was my sorry fate that hot August afternoon. A long suppressed, misdirected retaliation, perhaps, for having to stand there with a straight face for sixty-seven excruciating seconds.

Mercifully, not one other customer came in the store during this performance, or I would have lost it.

I never did find out how far up the pageant ladder she climbed, but she left delighted with her five outfits and contributed considerably to eliminating the poverty of a retail dog day in August.

"There are two kinds of people: those who come into a room and say, 'Well, here I am!' and those who come in andsay, 'Ah, there you are.'"

Frederick L. Collins

A Small Town Bride

Some customers never leave your heart. You greet them at the door, hear their stories, help them find a dress, take their measurements, order the dress, smile and weep a little with them as they stand for the first time in front of the mirror in their gown and veil. Then they're gone. And you're left to wonder.

Did the bride from Little Rock conquer her fear of moving to Hong-Kong with her new husband? Did the young divorced mother of two win over her future step-daughter? Did the bride with thyroid cancer beat the odds?

One such bride was Jenny, a wisp of a girl with copper red hair, trusting hazel eyes, and a flawless porcelain complexion. From the tiny Illinois town of Red Bud, population three-thousand-four-hundred and seventy-seven.

She was with her mother, was looking for a wedding gown, and was four and a half months pregnant.

Now, I know, for all you sophisticated readers living on the Sodom and Gomorrah coasts, this may not seem like a big deal. But, for most of us in the Red states of the Midwest, the accepted order of such things is still: engagement, marriage, pregnancy. Not pregnancy, engagement, marriage. At least in theory, if not always in practice.

Morality issues aside, Jenny and her mother were planning a full-scale church wedding with three hundred and fifty guests invited—one-tenth of the town's population. She had six bridesmaids and two flower girls and three months to pull it all off. Making her a full-blown eight months pregnant on her wedding day.

Sanny, a sales associate who had been with me forever, was helping Jenny try on wedding gowns when Jenny's mother pulled me aside and, fighting back tears, said, "I'm so happy for her. She's such a good girl and so in love. She was so frightened when she found out she was pregnant. Didn't even tell us until ten days ago. She even thought about ending the pregnancy. Thank God, she didn't. Tommy was terrified, too, but he loves Jenny and says he's ready to be a good father. Her father and I just want to support her and give her the wedding of her dreams. We'll pay any rush charges. Whatever she wants, we'll take care of it."

"Mom, look at this dress. Isn't it pretty? Do I look all right in it?"

"You look beautiful, Jenny, but I think you should try lots of them on. Anyway, I want to prolong this. It's so much fun. How will we ever decide? You're beautiful in everything you put on."

"Oh, Mom, you always say that. Do you think Tommy would like this one?"

"Absolutely. He loved that neckline on your prom dress. Really, Jenny, he's going to love the way you look no matter what dress you pick." "I hope so, Mom. Let's get serious about this one. I love it, but I wonder how it will look at eight months pregnant."

"Jenny," I said. "You've actually fallen for one of the best styles. The neckline will flatter your bustline, and the basque waist will help to conceal your expanding waistline. And don't forget your bouquet. When held strategically, it will help, too."

"That's right," she laughed, causing her hazel eyes to twinkle and a surprising dimple to appear in her right cheek. "I never thought about that. And it's not like this is a big secret. Everyone knows. Everyone's happy for me. I'm so lucky. What do you think, Mom?"

"I think it's a go. It's a gorgeous gown. The only problem is figuring out a size."

"That's our problem," I said. "We'll worry about that. Sanny will get your measurements today, and we'll estimate your weight gain. Our seamstress, Connie, is a wizard at handling any last minute alterations, so, not to worry."

"Great, then let's pick out my bridesmaid dresses. I've talked to all of them and together we've come up with the color and style they've agreed on. I want them all to feel comfortable and look pretty, and I've got their measurements, to save time."

Within fifteen minutes, mother and daughter had selected bridesmaid dresses in bright blue—a happy color, they said, for a happy event.

Two months later, Jenny drove in from Red Bud to try on the veil she had ordered and to pick out earrings and a necklace. She had the glow of full-blown pregnancy about her and a new matching dimple on her left cheek. We had all fallen in love with this waif of a bride who brought sunshine through the door each time she arrived.

Right on schedule, two weeks before the wedding, her gown arrived, and the following day, Jenny came in for the final fitting. No one was more surprised or delighted than me when she tried on her gown and it fit to perfection, with maybe a half an inch left in the waistband for those end of pregnancy pounds.

"I can't believe it, Mrs. Crowell. It's perfect. I've never felt so beautiful. Everything's going great. My bridesmaids love their dresses. The flowers are all on order, and we've received only a few regrets. Lots of people are coming from out of town, and our band's geared up for all night dancing.

"I went with Tommy to pick up his tux the other day. We still don't know if this baby is a girl or boy, but, if it's a boy, I hope he's as handsome as Tommy. Our priest is Tommy's uncle and has promised to baptize the baby too. So much going on, so much to be grateful for. Good grief, I'm carrying on too much!"

"No, you're not at all. We're all so happy for you, Jenny, and will be thinking of you all day on the nineteenth."

"Let's get you measured for the hem," Sanny said, "so it will be all ready to pick up on the eighteenth."

"Wonderful. My mom said she'd pick it up that day. We both want to thank you for all you've done. You've been great."

The morning of the eighteenth came and went, the afternoon slipping away with no one picking up Jenny's gown. Highway 40 backup, we thought.

At four-thirty, Jenny's mother came through the door, bringing no sunshine.

She told us that the day before, Tommy had told Jenny that he couldn't go through with the wedding. He was scared and not ready to be a husband or father. He had left town. A runaway groom. Jenny was devastated.

"Her bridesmaids have already flown in, lots of our guests from out of town are here, the food's being prepared, and the flowers are ready. We stayed up all last night, talking, crying and just hugging Jenny. Trying to figure out what to do.

"At about six-thirty this morning, Jenny said, 'My friends are all here. I have a gorgeous dress to wear and a beautiful baby coming soon. That's worth celebrating, so let's have a party.' So this wedding reception will be just that—a party. A party with lots of friends, family, good food and dancing. And Jenny will be fine. I know it."

I cry at weddings, I'll admit, but I had never cried over a cancelled wedding. And it wasn't only me. Sanny and I both sat down on the floor with a big box of Kleenex and just bawled.

Then we straightened up the shop, vacuumed the rug and locked the doors. Jenny, we prayed, would, indeed. be fine.

*"Things turn out best for the
people who make the best out
of the way things turn out."*

Art Linkletter

Sarah's Dream

*P*ractically every wedding I attended, people would come up to me and ask, "Why does anyone put themselves through all this work and trouble for just one day? Are they masochists? Why don't they use all that money toward a down payment on a house?"

These people are always called men.

First, it's not just one day. Showers, rehearsal dinners, spinster parties, etc., etc., are all part of it. Second, no, they're usually not masochists, although I've met a few.

And third, good point.

I would answer, "Because it's almost every girl's dream from the time her first fairytale is read to her."

The guy would walk away, shaking his head.

One of these dreamers was Sarah. She had been planning her wedding since she was seven years old and was well on her way to realizing that dream. She had a wedding planner, cathedral ceremony, country club reception, several bridesmaids, flower girls, ring bearers, a harpist—the whole works.

Her fiancé had been married before and had a been-there, done-that, don't-want-to-go-there-again frame of mind. And as things escalated (as they usually do) and stress mounted (as it usually does), he simply put his foot down.

And Sarah, wise Sarah, got the picture. She let go of the seven year old's dream and chose her man.

They were married on a beach in Florida with immediate family attending, and four children later, continue to grow in love and respect for each other. A beautiful thing to witness.

"I dreamed of a wedding of elaborate elegance,
A church filled with family and friends.
I asked him what kind of a wedding he wished for,
He said, one that would make me his wife."

Anonymous

Narciso Strikes

*B*ridal fashion in the early 1990s was pretty standard stuff. Pearls, lace, taffeta, ball gown skirts. Think Cinderella at the ball.

Then a young woman named Carolyn was married in an intimate, surprise ceremony on an island off the coast of Georgia. Her groom, for whom the word "hunk" was invented, was the son of a beloved President and affectionately known as John-John.

Working in secret was the designer Narciso Rodriguez, who, with this tall, slender, blonde beauty, a former public relations director at Calvin Klein, would revolutionize the bridal industry overnight.

Using a few yards of the finest, softest, ivory silk satin charmeuse, he would masterfully create a gown of such minimal chic that design house copiers would work seventy-two hours straight without sleep, fire many a pattern drafter and cutter, and be ready to throw themselves in front of a 7th Avenue bus trying to duplicate it. Of course, Narciso had the perfect body with which to work.

Madeline Vionnet, the French architect among dressmakers, had been prophetic in stating several decades before, "The dress must not hang on the body but follow its lines. It must accompany its wearer, and when a woman smiles, the dress must smile with her."

This nothing-to-it creation, when paired with delicate sandals and classic chignon, created a worldwide sensation as the never-to-be-forgotten photo of JFK, Jr., taking his bride's hand as she descended the steps of the little seaside chapel flashed across newspapers, magazines and TV screens everywhere.

Tragically, the magic ended much too soon. Senator Ted Kennedy's poignant words capturing the sorrow: they "had every gift but length of years."

The wedding had occurred on September 21, 1996. At the end of that September, sale racks in bridal stores across the country were crammed with pearl, lace and taffeta full-skirted bridal gowns. But everyone wanted to look like Carolyn. More precisely, everyone wanted to *be* Carolyn.

Designers scrambled to create look-alike slip gowns at every conceivable price point. Few succeeded. But, soon a more reasonable trend appeared. Gowns with tiny pearls scattered sparingly on the bodice; soft, flat Chanel bows at the shoulder, the only adornment on a satin slip dress; strapless A-line gowns with an overskirt of silk organza for interest. Understated elegance was back with a vengeance, and, for many a bridal store, it meant their demise. Very few had seen it coming.

Women were going to the gym for healthy, fit, trim bodies, and they didn't want to hide their efforts under layers and layers of fabric. The bridal industry would never be the same. The French have always understood this.

*"A dress makes no sense unless
it inspires men to want to
take it off you."*

Francoise Sagan

Prom Pitfalls

*O*ur disenchantment with prom season began around the fourth year after opening.

No matter what we brought in, it never seemed to be right. When I bought long gowns, everyone asked for short. When I bought short, they wanted long. Sometimes it felt like a high school conspiracy.

The main problem, I eventually figured out, was that this age group hadn't yet formed a sense of their own style. They either wanted a dress that looked like their best friend's, a dress they'd seen on the red carpet at the Academy Awards, or something guaranteed to bring about an argument with their mother.

Most mothers with any experience or savvy in this zany process, would wait until their darlings had been to at least seventy stores, had tried on a minimum of two hundred and ten dresses and had changed their minds at least fifteen times. Then, maybe then, it would be time to come in, bearing a credit card.

With Mom and credit card in tow, you'd think that decisions could be made.

Alas, dear reader, logic does not apply at prom time.

A typical exchange:

MOM: Becky, that's a beautiful dress on you. It brings out the color of your eyes.

BECKY: I think it makes my skin look green.

MOM: Maybe it comes in other colors.

BECKY: I wouldn't like it in another color.

MOM: Let's keep looking.

TWENTY-SEVEN DRESSES LATER.

BECKY: How about this strapless? Is it too revealing?

MOM: No, I don't think so.

BECKY: Let's find one with a lower neckline. It's too matronly.

MOM: Are you sure you want a long dress?

BECKY: No.

MOM: This little silver halter is pretty.

BECKY: They have that same dress down the street. Vicky tried it on and didn't like it.

MOM: It might look different on you. She's much taller.

BECKY: I know it, Mom. You don't have to rub it in. Why couldn't I have gotten some of that height? Wrong genes, I guess.

MOM: Let's not start that again, Becky. You're lucky to be who you are, healthy, with parents who love you.

BECKY: Health and love don't cut it when you're only five-foot-four and your date is six-foot-two.

MOM: We'll find some really high heels as soon as you pick out a dress. I really like the second one.

BECKY: It's okay.

MOM: For $395, it needs to be better than okay.

BECKY: Well, I guess I like it.

MOM: The price is right, it's great except for shortening the hem, and the color is lovely on you. So, let's do it.

CREDIT CARD POISED AND READY

BECKY: I'm just not sure yet. I think I want to start looking again. Maybe some of the stores down the street have gotten some new styles—something to make me look taller.

And so it went. And so it went. Until the following year, when we pulled the plug on prom. At the end of March, the high school darlings started showing up.

"Oh no, Mrs. Crowell. No prom dresses? Where are we going to go? You always knew what we wanted and had the best selection in town."

Retail lunacy.

"High heels were invented by a woman who had been kissed on the forehead."

Christopher Morley

Another Bride,
Another June

Outdoor weddings in St. Louis are not for the faint of heart. When they're good, they're very, very good, and when they're bad, they can be horrid. Both good and bad are defined as weather related.

"If you don't like the weather, wait a minute," is a truism in this town that no bride, mother, or wedding planner wants to hear.

"Another bride, another June,

Another sunny honeymoon," is still true and continues to be,

"Another reason,

For makin' whoopee."

Suzanne and her mother, following sixteen months of planning, seemed to have covered every contingency for the outdoor garden reception. A circus tent with Palladian eisenglass windows, three electric crystal chandeliers, air-conditioning for heat and humidity, heating for cold and humidity, a carpeted wood plank floor covering the interior of the tent, overhead fans to circulate the air, and, to keep it all going in case of a power outage, a massive generator.

Suzanne wanted the fairy tale dress and had selected a breathtaking strapless gown with a beaded bodice and an enormous layered tulle bouffant skirt—twenty-five layers of tulle by count. She wanted to float down the aisle and glide across the dance floor, giving the illusion of a gown propelled on its own power.

Her day arrived, sunny and resort like. The kind of weather that used to prompt my husband to say, "If it was like this year 'round, we couldn't afford to live here."

Mother Nature always seemed to have the last laugh though, and this wedding was no exception.

"You won't believe what happened. We thought we had everything under control," the mother-of-the-bride laughed, as she came into the store a week after the wedding. "The evening was going along so smoothly. Gorgeous weather and all. What we'd forgotten is that June is firefly month. Right around sundown, Suzanne started to notice little dots in her skirt. Fireflies and gnats were making their way up and in between all twenty-five layers of tulle. By the time it was dark, she was flickering off and on like the Eiffel Tower. People had never seen anything quite like it and were enchanted by the twinkling bride. I feel like we should pay you extra for the added feature of a shimmering skirt."

"That's a new one for us," I laughed. "Thanks for letting us know how it all went. I'll let you know if we get any brides coming in and asking for a twinkling skirt."

In this business, dear reader, you never know.

"Never wear anything that panics the cat."

P.J. O'Rourke

Drizella
And
Anastasia

*M*any Cinderellas walked through our door but we had only one Drizella and Anastasia. Regulars, I suppose you'd say, if you count purchasers of a few party dresses, a prom dress and a graduation dress as regular customers. In our business, you did.

They always came in with their mother—their stepsister undoubtedly left at home scrubbing the kitchen floor—and they always spent the first appointment trying on clothes, the second appointment placing an order and the third appointment questioning their decision. This round was for a debutante dress, an expensive outing.

Abigail, the oldest by two years, was a gangly five-foot-ten with straggly hair the color of motor oil, a Barbra Streisand nose, dry, cracked, thin lips coated unsuccessfully with a thick layer of Chapstick and dull brown eyes that were constantly surveying the ground in front of her. She appeared bored, never looked at me or anyone else when talking, and had what I called defeated posture.

A term I should know, because, at five-foot-ten-inches tall, going all the way back to the eighth grade, I, too, had defeated posture. But I had the solution. I was convinced that by bending my knees at a thirty-degree angle, thrusting my pelvis forward approximately three inches, sucking in my stomach until it appeared concave, slouching my shoulders forward and shortening my neck by tilting my chin down, I could give the illusion of being five-foot-six. A petite little thing. I was pregnant with my first child, and anatomically incapable of making my stomach appear concave, before I realized that all I had succeeded in doing all those years was to make myself look like a no-necked contortionist suffering from curvature of the spine. A five-foot-ten no-necked contortionist suffering from curvature of the spine.

Poor Abigail. I hoped it wouldn't take pregnancy for her to figure it out.

Sister Alice, on the other hand, was tiny and round and crabby. Her brown eyes darted everywhere, afraid, it seemed, that someone, Abigail perhaps, or Cinderella back home polishing that kitchen floor, was going to get something that she wasn't going to get. And she wasn't going to be caught off guard.

Not once had I seen these sisters smile. Hadn't they ever heard me preach that the most important thing you can wear when you enter a room is a smile? They were looking for a debutante dress when what they needed was an attitude adjustment.

"The plan," their mother was saying, "is for Abigail to wear the dress for this year's presentation and Alice to wear it two year's later for her presentation. So they both need to like it."

Aha, the picture was becoming clearer.

We'd helped several girls before to do this, but, most of the time, they had similar body types. These two couldn't have been farther apart in both height and weight. We'd just have to pull out another miracle with three-inch inseams and a deep hem, I thought, as I began to show them ball gowns from one of our finest designers, Chris Kole, known for his gowns worn on many a red carpet and gracing several films, Broadway musicals and television shows, including the Oscars and Grammy awards.

They liked several. I could tell because they said so. Their expressions didn't change.

Abigail liked the off-the-shoulder teal taffeta with lace around the bodice. Alice said no.

Alice liked the pale pink strapless satin with the wide beaded band at the waist. Abigail said no.

Abigail nixed the strapless green peau de soie. Alice concurred.

Abigail liked the off-the-shoulder aqua dupioni. Alice said maybe.

We were making progress.

"Let's have Alice try on the aqua dupioni," her mother said. "Abigail, you stay in that pink strapless. I'd like you both to stand side by side in these full-length mirrors, and we'll decide."

"Mirror, mirror on the wall…" kept going through my head.

Mom stood up and came to stand by me at the desk, so we could all get the best, and, theoretically, the same, view of Abigail and Alice.

Mom looked. On her right she saw a ravishing dark haired, willowy beauty, soon to be leaving the nest and captivating some handsome young unsuspecting bachelor she'd meet at the upcoming debutante ball. On her left she saw a beautiful little dumpling still under her wing to form into another beauty who would one day capture her own dashing bachelor. Both would soon provide her with dimpled, bouncing grandbabies and excuses to go shopping all over again for adorable baby outfits to show off to her bridge club.

Abigail looked and saw a too-tall, hook-nosed, soon-to-be college freshman, scared to death of leaving home and being thrust into a ballroom presentation with over three thousand people staring at her.

Alice looked and saw an off-shoulder aqua dupioni gown with at least six inches of extra skirt fabric puddling at her feet, a neckline falling off her shoulders and a dress that would be two years old, worn and probably red wine stained by the time she wore it.

I looked and saw Drizella and Anastasia.

Amazing how mirrors can give back so many different reflections of the same image. Don't they ever think before they reflect?

A purchase was made. The aqua dupioni. I think they were happy. I hope they were happy. I really couldn't tell.

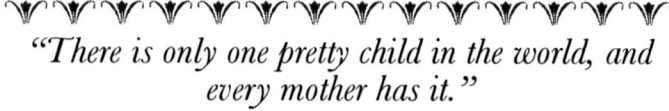

"There is only one pretty child in the world, and every mother has it."

Chinese proverb

Ladue

I grew up in Ladue (pronounced "La-doo"), and lived there from the age of two until I was married.

It was a sleepy, graceful, tree-lined small town with two lane, narrow roads, often shared with forest green Schwinn bicycles, tan wicker baskets strapped to the front handlebars.

There was the Ladue Pharmacy, where you could buy anything from a package of Camels, a girdle or a vacuum cleaner to a used Studebaker. Prices negotiable. Various and sundry remedies were also offered that promised to keep residents free of everything from poison ivy itch, arthritis pain, heartburn and constipation to the heartbreak of psoriasis.

Down the road a bit was the Ladue Market, where butchers actually spoke to you, remembered what you had served for dinner the night before, and, with a wink and a smile, would suggest a menu for the evening's meal. Customers said, "Excuse me," backed up their carts and waited until you'd made your selection of either Del Monte or Heinz canned peas before entering the twenty-one inch wide aisle for their own canned pea search.

Locally grown fresh peaches were fuzzy and juicy when in season, and tomatoes came in irregular shapes and sizes and varied shades of red—and tasted like tomatoes. A portly young man would carry out your groceries and load them into your red Ford Country Squire station wagon, saying, "Thanks for coming in, Mrs. Carmichael. I hope Mr. Carmichael's gout isn't acting up these days. Maybe you shouldn't have bought those sardines. Take care, and I'll see you tomorrow."

When you didn't feel like cooking, Busch's Grove was right across the street from Ladue Market and *the* place to go. Since 1893, when travelers in stagecoaches would stop to fortify themselves, this large white frame building with the wide front porch had been a local gathering spot. A kind of no-dues, no-membership, no-frills country club. Known for its hefty double scotch and waters, mediocre food, less than attentive service and outdoor wooden cabin huts on the back patio, its motto was, "All roads lead to Busch's Grove."

Some of my fondest childhood memories are of fried chicken dinners with my mother, father, two brothers and baby sister (in her high chair). Just the six of us in our private screened-in hut. Overhead fan humming, kamikaze June bugs dive bombing the screens, flashes of heat lightning streaking across the western sky, and hot fudge sundaes in frosty chilled tin cups topping off all this wonderment.

Half a mile west of Busch's Grove was the Catholic church, Annunziata, at that time a mere chapel in the living room of the home of Father Farris, one of the gentlest men I've ever known. When not saying Mass, comforting the sick or giving solace in the confessional, he could be seen tilling, planting and weeding the half-acre garden he cultivated west of his house. Frequently he was mistaken for the gardener, and he relished the telling of it.

I made my First Communion in this cozy living room chapel and would be married years later in a grand stone church, to be built by his successor, right smack over Father Farris' lovingly tended radishes, beets and rhubarb.

Ladue School was a climb over a five-foot fence and a mile away on foot no matter what the weather. The library required a four-minute ride in a rickety orange bus that ran when it felt like it and, when so inclined, would also drop you off at Gutman's, the two-story department store, where you could find Bermuda shorts, cashmere twin-sets, the softest cloth diapers in town, and, most exciting of all, an X-ray machine in the shoe section where you could stick your feet inside and see your bones.

The one gas station on Ladue Road was full service, the only kind of service people were aware of in those days. The overall clad attendants came running out, filled your car up for about twenty cents a gallon, kicked your tires to make sure they had enough air, checked your oil, cashed a check if you needed it and filled you in on all the latest gossip on your street. Rumor had it that the owner, Steve, offered a few other services, which shall remain nameless.

It was a laid back town from Sunday night to Friday, but when Friday night rolled around it was time to party. And I do mean party. Which meant party dresses. *The* place to go for party dresses was a small shop called Elsa Brady's, a red brick establishment with dark green awnings in front, shading window displays of beautiful dresses sold by kind and welcoming women. My mother, a classic beauty with impeccable style, always took me there to shop. Little did she know then that she was setting in motion the ambience and philosophy of selling that I would put in place some twenty years later, when opening my own shop.

Twenty years later, when my business was launched, Ladue was still a sleepy, graceful, tree-lined small town, with two lane narrow roads. Gone were Gutman's, Elsa Brady's, the Ladue Road gas station and twenty-cent-a-gallon gasoline. Schwinn bikes were being replaced by Fezzari road bikes, red Ford Country Squire station wagons by BMWs, and Ladue Pharmacy was no longer selling used Studebakers. The population had jumped to almost eight thousand, housing prices had skyrocketed, and the median income had become one of the highest of any city in the United States.

Long-time residents took this all in stride. Newcomers and non-residents frequently did not. Some developed an attitude—an "I'm just as cool as you are, so don't give me any guff just because you're a Ladue old timer" attitude. I saw it all over town and shouldn't have been surprised when it walked into my shop.

As soon as I saw it coming, and it was pretty easy to spot, I would start to pour on the kindness, launching an offensive counterattack before any chip on the shoulder could develop. It became a game I relished playing, and it always worked in our favor.

No need to play the game when long-time residents Ginny Schneider and her daughter Julia came in. They were planning what would turn out to be one of the largest, most elaborate weddings in St. Louis, with a ceremony at the St. Louis Cathedral and reception at the Ritz. It was the social event of the early 1990s. For us, it turned out to be one of the easiest, most pleasant experiences we ever had. Mutual courtesy and respect always prevail.

A week after the wedding, I received a call from the bride's mother. "I just wanted to call and tell you how much we enjoyed working with all of you and how happy we were with the way everything turned out. Thank you so much."

"You're very welcome," I said. "How nice of you to call."

"The only blip came at the reception. I think I told you that Julia collects Lladro figurines. Well, I surprised her with a Lladro bride and groom for the top of her wedding cake. Shortly before it was time for them to cut the cake, the photographer was backing up to get a photo of Julia and Tony dancing and didn't see the cake table. I was across the room and saw what was going to happen but couldn't do anything about it. He kept backing up and backing up—bumped into the table—knocked over the Lladro bride and groom—and decapitated them!"

She laughed, "I just walked over, picked up their heads, went into the kitchen, found some instant glue and glued them back on. None the worse for wear, and Julia never knew the difference. She's not superstitious, but I thought a bride and groom should at least have their heads attached on their wedding day. All in all though, it was perfect. Thanks so much."

Calm mother, calm bride. A win-win combination and the best kind of attitude.

"God gave you a gift of 86,400 seconds today.
Have you used one to say, 'Thank you'?"

William A. Ward

The Freshman Fifteen

*F*ew words instill greater fear into a graduating high school senior's psyche than *freshman fifteen*. Leaving home? Big deal. Cash shortfall? MasterCard. Psycho roommate? Won't happen. No car? Enterprise. All night study session? Starbucks. Freshman fifteen? AARRGGHHHHH!

You might as well take those pepperoni pizza slices and laminate them right smack onto their hips. Take the ubiquitous quarts of amber beer and siphon it out of the kegs right smack onto their nubile, hourglass waistlines. And if pizza and beer don't do it, surely cafeteria food will.

Hillary Reston, a high school senior and regular customer, came in with her mother looking for a debutante gown to be worn over the Christmas holidays of her freshman year at college. Her destination: Stanford.

The dress code for this debutante ball was strict: no strapless, no cleavage, no hip-hugging skirts. Gowns had to be white, full skirted, floor length, and worn with traditional elbow length, white kidskin gloves with pearl buttons.

"My mom and I have been looking forward to this for a long time, Mrs. Crowell. I see at least a dozen dresses I'd like to try on. Let's start."

Mom sat in the delicate white wicker armchair, next to the "Kleenex table," strategically placed for mothers viewing their daughters in a long white dress for the first time. Hillary paraded back and forth, in and out of the dressing room.

"Mom, I look just like Scarlett O"Hara in this. Remember the scene where Prissy whines, 'Miz Scarlett, you ain't neva' gonna' have no eighteen-inch waist again. You done jus' had a baby.'

"And look at this one with all the beading. Too bridal? How about this puckered ball gown skirt? Janie and Joey and their entire kindergarten class could hide under here.

"Here's one I really like. What do you think?"

"I agree, Hillary. It's a bit pricey but your father will be escorting you, and he wants you to have a dress you love. Let's get you measured. I think we've found the right dress to order."

As I took Hillary's measurements, she reminded me, "Mrs. Crowell, I won't be coming home at all between the day I arrive at Stanford and the night of the ball. I'll pick up my dress two days before."

"I'll alert our seamstress, and any last minute alterations can be done two days before. We've done this before. Just don't do the freshman fifteen."

She didn't. She did the freshman fifty.

Two days before the ball, I received a call from Hillary's mother, coming home from picking up her daughter at the airport and seeing her for the first time since August. "Uhh, Judy, we have a problem."

Webster's dictionary defines the word *gusset* as "a piece of armor covering the joints in a suit of armor; a triangular insert (as in a seam of a sleeve) to give width or strength."

Fortunately, we were dealing with the latter and, as always, had mountains of white silk satin fabric stored in the stock room. Our on-alert seamstress located a yard or so of matching fabric and within twenty-four hours Hillary was "gusseted" up and ready for a proud father to present his Botticelli beauty at the Christmas ball.

Hillary returned to Stanford, a wiser second-semester freshman and by the end of her sophomore year was back to her athletic, healthy, pre-beer, pre-pizza self.

"I've been on a constant diet for the last two decades. I've lost a total of 789 pounds. By all accounts, I should be hanging from a charm bracelet."

Erma Bombeck

What Queen Victoria Started

How many dresses should a bride try on before finding her wedding gown? Two? Seven? A dozen? Twenty-five? Sixty? One hundred and ten?

In 1840, Queen Victoria broke with tradition by choosing a white gown for her wedding to Albert. Two hundred needlewomen were sequestered for eight months fashioning an eighteen-foot train, a veil trimmed with orange blossoms and a magnificent gown designed to match the Queen's favorite pieces of white lace.

Since then, countless brides have dreamed and agonized over their own perfect white gown, and reams and reams of advice have been expounded in weighty bridal magazines. Fantasy slicks featuring anorexic fourteen-year-old models in contortionist poses, with sassafras twigs for hair, unicorns peering out from behind banyan trees, turreted castles on the horizon ostensibly housing the Prince-Charming-Soon-To-Be-Bridegroom, and gowns so heavily laden with beading that one would be lucky to be able to rise off the moss covered tree trunk, let alone walk down the aisle of a church.

Advice ad nauseam:

- Take your best friend with you for an honest opinion. (Give me a break.)
- Take your camera, and be sure to ask if photos are permitted. (Good luck.)
- Do not go out for lunch immediately before your bridal appointment. (Duh.)

- Set your budget beforehand and stick to it. (Never happens.)
- Learn about laces: cluny, schiffli, alencon, chantilly, Venice, wedgewood, re-embroidered, etc., etc., etc.
- Learn about trains: chapel, cathedral, watteau, sweep, royal, semi, etc., etc., etc.
- Learn about necklines: halter, sweetheart, portrait, sabrina, scoop, U-shaped, V-neck, illusion high, bateau…

Enough already!

There are sleeves, headpieces, veils and the all-important silhouettes still to consider.

Silhouette advice can be summed up thusly: Accentuate the positive and eliminate the negative. Or, to be more specific:

- A-line skirts conceal a multitude of hip issues.
- An empire silhouette hides a thick waist.
- Bateau necklines flatter a flat-chested bride.
- Skinny brides should avoid skinny straps and low necklines.
- Bodacious brides bode well in sweetheart necklines and basque waists.
- Swimmers with broad shoulders will look good in strapless gowns.

Blah, blah, blah, blah, blah.

My all time, personal favorite is, "You'll just know. Don't worry, you'll just know."

I can't tell you how many fretful brides have come to me with those sappy words of wisdom ringing in their susceptible little ears. Stepping into the dressing room, slipping into the white satin heels provided, sucking in their butterfly-filled tummies as satin after satin gown is eased over their trembling torsos. Breathlessly awaiting a sign. Any sign. A blush of their cheeks. An aura of serenity. A halo around their head—or, the salesperson's head. Hives. Their mother and maid-of-honor breaking into sobs and making a mad dash for the strategically placed Kleenex box. The sun coming out from behind the clouds. A rainbow. A choir of angels singing.

I kid you not.

The saddest part of all is that often a bride *will* find the perfect dress, but not realize it until several months later, when it's no longer available.

"But, Mrs. Crowell, nothing really happened to me in the fitting room. I loved the dress, the fit, the style, the way I looked, the way it made me feel. I knew my fiancé would love it on me. It was the right price. Everything was perfect. But nothing else happened."

This bride, patient, reader, was/is the quintessence of The Bride Who Tries on Too Many Dresses.

One can't help but wondering if the same process of elimination was utilized in selecting the groom.

"*Dress is at all times a frivolous distinction, and excessive solicitude about it often destroys its own aim.*"

Jane Austen

Zip-a-dee-doo-dah

Zippers are a marvelous invention and do what they are designed to do 99.9% of the time.

Infants are swaddled in fluffy buntings, zipped up to their rosy cheeks before venturing out on snowy winter days. Toddlers delight in the game of zipping up and down, down and up, discovering the shock value, freedom and exhilaration of birthday suits. Teens take the invention to levels never intended, wriggling into skin tight designer jeans, and women, without a passing thought, trust them every day to bend, stretch and stay aligned in their coils from sunrise to sunset. Men, of course, rely heavily on zippers. Sad to say, history is rife with tales of "gentlemen" who couldn't learn to keep their zippers zipped. Rituals have come a long way since Roman times, when grooms would anticipate untying knots tied in a girdle worn by the bride on her wedding day. Thus, the phrase, "tying the knot."

Betsy was going to be a gorgeous bride. Our shop was outfitting most of her wedding party with the wedding gown, veil, bridesmaid dresses, MOB dress and six flower-girl dresses. My daughter, one of the bride's best friends, was a bridesmaid, and the wedding, to which I had been invited, was to take place in the same church where my husband and I had been married some forty years before.

The cornflower blue of the bridesmaids' dresses matched the bright blue June sky, like a cloudless summer sky walking down the aisle. MOB was radiant, flower girls precious and Betsy breathtaking in her heavily beaded alencon lace off-the-shoulder gown.

Bride and groom stood hand in hand at the altar, listening to the violin strains of Pachelbel's Canon, their backs to three-hundred-plus guests. Immediately before the second reading, Corinthians, chapter 13, verses 1–13, I thought I spied movement in the middle of the bride's three-thousand-dollar wedding gown.

"If I should speak with the tongues of men and of angels, but do not have love, I have become as sounding brass or a tinkling cymbal. And if…."

I *knew* I had seen movement on her gown.

Slowly, oh so slowly, I watched as the zipper began to spread apart. Was I the only one aware of it?

"Love is patient; love is kind; love does not envy, is not pretentious…" the reader intoned.

Oh, God, I prayed. *Bless this couple, give them children and peace in their old age, and, please dear God, don't let that damn zipper go any lower.*

Well, two beautiful babies have since arrived and the peace in their old age part remains to be seen. But God did not hear my prayer about the zipper. Probably, in the scheme of things, He had better things to do.

Undaunted, it slowly slithered waistward, quarter inch by quarter inch, until the maid-of-honor and my bridesmaid daughter became aware of what was happening and tried as unobtrusively as possible to lift the bridal veil and zip the zipper back up, unfortunately neglecting to hook the hook at the top of the zipper, which probably would have prevented the trauma in the first place.

I must say, it did make for a most entertaining and suspenseful ceremony.

A quick repair by securing the hook and eye at the top of the zipper saved the day, and soon they were off in a horse drawn carriage to their reception, to dance the night away and laugh about the up and down beginning of their married life.

On rainy days, three year old, Tommy, loves to sit in front of the TV and watch the video of Mommy's sliding zipper on that glorious June day when all the things that really mattered went very right.

Zip-a-dee-doo-dah, what a wonderful day!

"A dress that zips up the back will bring a husband and wife together."

James H. Boren

Sticky Fingers

𝕏 *W*hen it came to security, we ran one of the loosiest-goosiest operations along our tony suburban shopping strip. Remember, we were a Cheers kind of place, where everybody knew your name, and, to the best of our knowledge, no one who walked through our doors had ever spent any time in the big house for grand larceny.

Then, one particularly busy afternoon, right after my daughter, Kim, and I were rummaging around for a size 6 dress for a size 12 customer (the customer is always right, trusting reader), we returned to the show-room and realized that two of our best "diamond" watches had disappeared from the jewelry case. Also gone was a customer who'd been looking for earrings. A wife, mother and grandmother. A pillar of the community. A Mrs. Sticky Fingers.

Kim was so angry to have our open atmosphere violated that she was ready to jump in her car and track this "respectable" bandit down.

With no witnesses to the crime and no DNA, I was a bit concerned about possible charges of defamation of character, false arrest, lack of evidence. All those technical little hurdles we'd have to face from Mrs. Sticky Finger's defense attorney (no less than an O.J./Johnny Cochran/Robert Shapiro type) during the months-long criminal trial that would ensue and be covered in searing detail by every local TV station, possibly being picked up by the *Today Show*.

So we compromised. Kim did not give chase. She sent her a bill. So direct. So simple. And, wonder of wonders, six days later, we received a check for $878.56 and a thank-you note right out of Emily Post's Etiquette Book, 17th Edition:

> Thank you for your help in showing me these lovely watches and for allowing me to take them home on approval to show my husband. He suggested that I keep them both since I can't decide which one I like the best.
>
> Sincerely,
> Mrs. Sticky Fingers

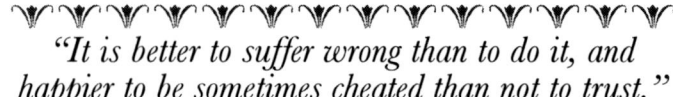

"It is better to suffer wrong than to do it, and happier to be sometimes cheated than not to trust."

Samuel Johnson

A Weighty Issue

*W*ould you believe, dear reader, that everyone who walked through our doors had the same last name? We had Jennifers, Mollys and Lindseys. Dozens of Sarahs, Carols and Debbies. A handful of Ruths, one or two Beth Anns and a Lucretia. All walked in saying, "Hi, I'm 'Mary' Imgoingtolosetwentypoundsbynextmonth." A mouthful of a moniker.

Brides often did drop five to ten pounds right before the wedding, thanks to a combination of endless bottles of Evian water, sushi and nerves.

MOBs and MOGs usually managed to add a few pounds, thanks to bridal showers featuring wine, chicken salad, caramel rolls and euphoria.

Bridesmaids frequently grew outwardly, a nine-month bump, and flower girls grew upwards.

Determining sizes was a weighty issue, a crapshoot at best. But one we solved, more often than not, by convincing the many Imgoingtolosetwentypoundsbynextmonths that they looked pretty darned fantastic just the way they were. Then adding an inch or two to each seam measurement.

*"The biggest seller is cookbooks
and the second is diet books:
how not to eat what you just learned to cook."*

Andy Rooney

A Slippery Slope

*B*ridezilla (brīd/ZIL/uh): n. A bride-to-be who, while planning for her wedding, becomes exceptionally selfish, greedy and obnoxious.

Over 447,000 Bridezilla Websites exist, weekly episodes of the reality show, *Bridezilla*, can be endured on the Women's Entertainment Network, and in 1999, *Modern Bride* magazine launched a Bridezilla comic strip.

The phenomenon of Bridezilla, relatively new, strikes terror in many a bridal consultant. We certainly had our share. Perfectly normal women, metamorphosed into monsters the moment that two-karat rock is placed on their fourth finger.

Most alarming, future husbands are oblivious until it's too late.

It's a slippery slope, this slide down the rose petal strewn path of bridal insanity, but there are some warning signs along the way to tell if you qualify as a Bridezilla. Here are just a few.

- Your favorite florist calls to tell you that they're planning to close for inventory control two days before your wedding.
- Your pharmacist triples your dosage of Zoloft, without a prescription.
- Your five-year-old niece and flower girl breaks out in hives whenever you appear.
- Your sister and matron-of-honor disconnects her phone, legally changes her name, and moves to Canada.

- The skin on your ring finger turns green.
- Stacks of bridal magazines block your doorways and become a fire hazard.
- Flyers for mail order, one-size-fits-all straight jackets appear in your mailbox.
- Your boss suggests a vacation, preferably permanent.
- Your father takes out a third mortgage on the house.
- Your mother develops a facial tic and exhibits other signs of an impending nervous breakdown.

Two out of ten positive responses: you may still be able to salvage some dignity. Four out of ten: Houston, we have a problem. You need professional, psychiatric help. Six out of ten: forget it. Just look up "divorce lawyers" in the Yellow Pages, or, better still, give the bling-bling back to the poor sucker and save yourself, your intended and others who may or may not still love you, the trouble of showing up on your wedding day.

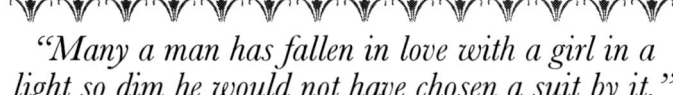

"Many a man has fallen in love with a girl in a light so dim he would not have chosen a suit by it."

Maurice Chevalier

Gideon Sunback

*N*ot exactly a household name, this Gideon Sunback fellow, but every time you get dressed in the morning and zip up your slacks, every time you reach back to unzip a little black cocktail dress, you have this Swedish-born scientist to thank for inventing the zipper.

Patented in 1913 as the "Hookless Fastener," it was defined as "a fastening device consisting of parallel rows of metal, plastic or nylon teeth on adjacent edges of an opening that are interlocked by a sliding tab."

The idea didn't quite take off in popularity. Many were skeptical, and the clergy didn't help at all. Condemning the contraptions as "devil's work," allowing wearers to remove their clothes too quickly, thereby aiding and abetting illicit sexual activity.

Not until the end of World War II did the zipper spread throughout the world, showing up in everything from luggage and pencil cases to space suits and galoshes.

Like electricity, telephones and fax machines, the lowly zipper is taken for granted, not given a second thought until it doesn't work.

Over the years, we sold thousands of special occasion dresses. Five or six, at the most, had defective zippers. Not a pleasant experience if you happened to be one of those five or six. Two, including Betsy, were brides. Two or three were bridesmaids, and one was a debutante from Springfield, Missouri, attending the town's Snowflake Ball.

A week after the holiday charity ball, I received a call from across state from the young lady's mother. "Hello, Mrs. Crowell, I wanted to talk to you about Susan's dress."

"How was it? I hope she had a great time." I replied.

"She did, but the weather was awful. It rained all night long. We've had nothing but lousy weather for as long as I can remember, and there was no snow for the Snowflake Ball."

"Well, good thing it was all indoors. I hear that the decorations and flowers were spectacular this year. I'll bet she looked beautiful."

"She did, I guess. She'd been looking forward to this night since she was two years old and since she's our only child, it had to be a perfect night. She had pictures taken before the presentation. I don't know where they found the photographer, but he was a mess and kept us waiting twenty minutes. Susan had to stand up the entire time to keep her dress from wrinkling. She said she'd never felt so pretty as when she was presented. I guess she did look okay, but we were seated on the left side of the room instead of the right side as I had requested. Her right side has always been her best side."

"Really?" I said.

"Yes. Even her boyfriend agrees. He was seated on the right side. But my reason for calling is to tell you that after she was presented, right before dinner, the zipper on her gown broke, and she was beside herself. Here it was, the most important night in her life, one she'd been dreaming about for sixteen years, and the night was ruined. Ruined."

"Oh, I'm so sorry. What did she do?"

"I walked behind her so no one could see that the zipper was broken, and we went to the hospitality room where a seamstress was on call who had to sew her into the dress.

It took about fifteen minutes, so she missed part of the dinner and returned to the ballroom in a state of shock. The whole time she was dancing, I was terrified it would split again."

"What a terrible experience for her. I'm so sorry it happened, but it sounds like most of the evening was successful."

"Successful?!? How can you even suggest that? It was the worst experience of her life. How would you feel if that happened to you? Or to your daughter? You wouldn't be so flippant if it had happened to someone in your family. I don't know if she'll ever get over this. My husband and I expect a full refund on the price of her gown. I made sure that everyone at the ball knew where the dress had come from and warned everyone I could about buying from you in the future."

A few more ridiculous exchanges transpired, and I soon realized that nothing short of my beheading was going to satisfy this distraught mother.

Grinding my teeth and counting to ten, I apologized sincerely once again, told her a check would be in the mail, and expressed my hope that this traumatizing life experience would be the worst thing ever to happen to her daughter.

A week later, I discovered that our seamstress, a month prior to the Snowflake Ball, had replaced the original zipper on Susan's gown with an invisible zipper, pronouncing the original one defective. Big mistake.

Invisible zippers have become the darlings of the evening gown and bridal industry. Made usually of polyester, they are produced in a huge array of colors (think paint charts), so that the color of the gown can be matched to the zipper. Thus making them "invisible" except for the slider. A lovely idea, except that frequently they don't work.

Imagine taking a layer of poly silk lining fabric, a second layer of interfacing, another layer of beaded lace and a final layer of silk satin and jamming them all into a back or side seam with a $1.25 invisible zipper, expecting them to keep you intact and zipped up throughout the hugging and kissing of wedding guests, dancing the Macarena or chicken dance and tossing your bouquet to a pre-arranged, forty-two-year-old spinster. I'm not saying they never work. I'm just saying, would you want to be the one or two or three or four or five wearing the gown with the zipper that splits apart? Personally, I think that industrial zippers are a great choice for some of the gyrations debs and brides go through these days.

So many zippers. So many different kinds. And so many varied reactions to their indiscretions.

Gideon, you old devil, look what you started.

"It's snowing still," said Eeyore gloomily.
"So it is." "And freezing." "Is it?" "Yes," said
Eeyore. "However," he said, brightening
up a little, "we haven't had an earthquake lately."

A. A. Milne

Bust, Waist
And Hips

𝒳 *W*ithout a doubt, the trickiest part of our business involved orders for bridesmaid dresses. Forms requiring name, address, phone number, height, weight, bust, waist, hip measurements and an innocuous double line requesting *other information* were faxed, emailed, snail mailed and phoned in to us from all over the world. We never laid eyes on half of our bridesmaids.

Typical planning for a December wedding went something like this:

- January: Bride begins search for bridesmaid dresses.
- April: Bride finalizes selection.
- May: Brides asks bridesmaids to send in measurements or come in to be measured.
- August: Bridal boutique places order with dress designers.
- October: Dresses arrive and are either shipped to or picked up by bridesmaids.
- November: Alterations are completed.

This, of course, was the ideal scenario. All sorts of snags could and did occur during that eleven-month period, many falling under the nebulous heading of *other information.* Snags such as:

- Change of address.
- Weight loss.
- Weight gain.
- Termination of services by bride.
- Defections under the Bridesmaid Witness Protection Program.

- Illness.
- Death.

And the number one snag, our all time favorite…

- Pregnancy.

Here are just a few samples of replies received on those two dreaded blank lines marked *other information:*

- "I'm six foot, two inches tall and the bride wants us to wear three-inch heels. Please order my skirt long enough to cover my shoes so no one will see that I'm wearing flats."
- "The bride either forgot or doesn't care that my religion doesn't allow me to wear anything that shows my arms and chest. What should I do?"
- "My bust measurement should be a lot smaller by the time of the wedding since I'm having a breast reduction in June. How many inches should I take off this measurement?"
- "My bust measurement should be a lot larger by the time of the wedding since I'm having a breast enhancement in June. How many inches should I add to this measurement?"
- From Ashley in Mobile, Alabama: "I think a mistake has been made here. Yes, I'm the maid-of-honor for my sister Mary, but I won't be needing a dress. I'm her brother."
- "I like to wear my clothes tight. The bride always looks like she's wearing a sack. Please order my dress the way I like it, not the way she likes it."

- "I can't believe the bride picked this color. I'm going to have to buy all new make-up so I don't look like a corpse."
- "I live in London now but am moving to Israel for six weeks in August. Then to Newfoundland for October before flying to Australia in November. Send my dress to my mother in California so I can get it altered there the week before the wedding. She'll FedEx it overnight to the bride in St. Louis."
- "I just had a baby so these measurements are way off. Please deduct three inches off the waist and hip measurement. I'll keep nursing so my bust will look good in the strapless dress."
- "I'm ordering my matron-of-honor dress to be worn three times. I'll wear it at the wedding, my oldest daughter will wear it for prom, and my twelve-year-old daughter for her father/daughter dance. My measurements: 38/32/39; prom daughter: 40/33/41; twelve year old: 28/26/28. What size should I order?"
- From Sunbeam in Petaluma, California: "I respectfully refuse to order. The only thing I allow to cover my body is biodegradable clothing made of pesticide free fabric. I will inform the bride of my decision the day of the wedding."
- "Be sure to put ATTENTION SUPER on the

outside of the package. The landlord's Great Dane has eaten up several UPS packages in the last month."

And our all-time favorite, which happened again and again and again, never ceasing to crack us up:

- "My husband and I are trying to get pregnant. What should we do?"

Now, savvy reader, when this inquiry came in over the phone, which it often did, I had to take a deep breath and bite my tongue to keep from saying what I really wanted to say: "Well, dear, you prepare a nice candlelit dinner, preferably with oysters somewhere on the menu, go to Victoria's Secret and find the skimpiest little black lacey thing in the store, run home, put it on and then take that handsome hunk of a hubby of yours by the hand up the stairs to your bedroom and let nature take its course."

I didn't.

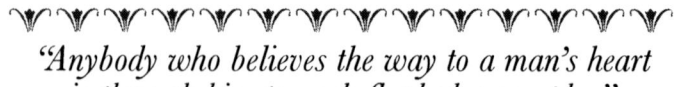

"Anybody who believes the way to a man's heart is through his stomach flunked geography."

Robert Byrne

To Veil Or Not To Veil

*B*y far, the most contentious item of apparel we dealt with was the veil.

Brides under twenty-five loved them, especially when topped with a diamond tiara. Between the ages of twenty-five and thirty, opinions varied according to what Brittany, Heather or Sophia had worn at the most recently attended wedding. After thirty, forget it. No amount of tears shed by a doting mother, finally getting her dumpling daughter to the altar, would bully her daughter into masquerading as a blushing bride.

Superstitions surrounding veils range from good luck befalling the bride whose veil is accidentally ripped at the altar to bad luck plaguing the bride who permits anyone other than a happily married woman to place the veil on her head or to style her hair for the wedding. (This pretty much eliminates eight-five percent of the hair stylists I know.)

The custom of the bridal veil dates back to the Roman Empire, when bright red or yellow veils were worn to ward off evil spirits. Spirits believed to be poised and ready to pounce on the innocent maiden, whisking her away before being able to wed her betrothed. The word "nuptial" comes from the Latin word *nubo* which means, "I veil myself."

During the Middle Ages, the Crusaders introduced the veil to European cultures, which was a very convenient addition to their practice of arranged marriage. Designed to completely conceal, brides were swathed in a veil and revealed to their husbands only after the ceremony, when, presumably, the poor blokes were trapped.

President George Washington's niece was the first American bride to wear a veil for her wedding. Her fiancé, such a gallant guy, had seen her face through a lace curtain and was dazzled by how beautiful she looked. In some circles this would be considered a back-door compliment.

Two world wars brought frugality to the wedding scene, to the point of shortening wedding gowns to above-knee length in the front during the 1920s, all in an effort to conserve fabric. With the advent of nylon, following World War II, sheer, billowy veils of tulle became popular and remain so today.

Current styles include cathedral, chapel, ballet, waltz, wreath and mantilla. Several are self-explanatory: fingertip (ending at your fingertips), elbow (ending at your elbows), sweep (sweeping the floor), birdcage (attached to a headpiece and enclosing your face), flyaway (it does), and angel cut (giving you the illusion of angel wings as you walk down the aisle. Grooms love that last one—*not.*

Veils can be bright white, diamond white, ivory, ecru and tea stained. The darker the veil, the drearier the complexion. The brighter the veil, the sallower the complexion. Diamond white, a winner, was our bestseller.

Veils could be edged with anything from a thin cording to wide satin ribbon and sprinkled with everything from tiny Swarovski crystals to silk flowers.

Having purchased a tulle veil scattered with eight millimeter pearls from a competitor of ours, a lovely bride was horrified when her photos came back from the photographer. Opting to wear her pearl embellished veil as a blusher over her face, every photo prior to the exchange of vows made her look like she had a terminal case of the pox. Over-the-face veils, or blushers, should never, ever have beading on them.

Likewise, a cathedral length veil of some one hundred and ten inches shouldn't be worn for a beach wedding: danger of seaweed tangle. Fly-away veils aren't advised for mountain top exchange of vows: they'll do it. And waltz veils don't work well if your first dance is to be a tango.

No two veils are alike. They are as numerous as the stars in the heavens.

Tired of hearing about veils, patient reader? My sentiments exactly, the entire time I sold them.

However, silly old romantic that I am, I still find few things more stirring than a young bride, her expectant, trusting face veiled in illusion, surrounded by the love of family and friends, walking down the aisle towards the man she will promise to love and cherish for the rest of her life.

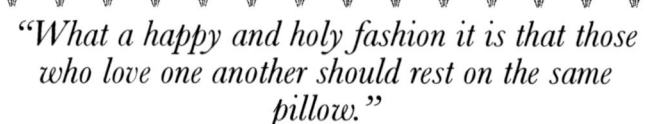

"What a happy and holy fashion it is that those who love one another should rest on the same pillow."

Nathaniel Hawthorne

Future In-laws

$\mathcal{H}$ *T*here are some things that are so outrageously predictable that one despairs of wasting breath to tell or pen and ink to write of such folly. Such as:

- Walking into the examining room of your doctor's office, thermostat set at sixty-two degrees and being told by the nurse to remove all your clothes and cover yourself with a white modesty sheet having the consistency of Kleenex. The doctor will be in shortly.

- Taking a six-foot ladder outside to Windex away the bird droppings on your eleven-foot-high bay window. Climbing up to the second highest rung, one rung past the warning label, and feeling the back bottom feet of the ladder sink into the gopher softened ground. (My orthopedic surgeon would have to fill you in on the aftermath of this one. I don't remember anything past seeing a cloudless, blue sky and treetops passing overhead.)

- Childless child bride, your baby sister, ordering an all white linen Eton suit for your four-and-a-half-year-old son, her nephew, to wear as a ring bearer at her country wedding in April. Rainy season. The ceremony scheduled for one o'clock in the afternoon with the reception at six o'clock in the evening. (One of those "split" affairs.) Since there is no place to change clothes, guests and all-white linen clad four-and-a-half-year-old boy must remain in wedding attire for the five-hour interim. For-mal photos of the wedding party, ring bearer included, are to take place by the bass-stocked lake between five and six o'clock. Childless child bride plans to give your son a fishing rod and a can of worms so he can "fish off the dock, have lots of fun and, in years to come, look back fondly at how spiffy he looked in his immaculate white linen suit."

This is one of those stories, and, as such, I will try to keep it brief.

FIRST APPOINTMENT: Bride arrives looking for eight bridesmaid dresses. Informs us that her future sister-in-law is very overweight, rather unattractive (this proved an understatement), had never been a brides-maid (or bride) and that it was exceedingly important for her to be made to feel comfortable and pretty.

SECOND APPOINTMENT: Bride returns with MOB to view her four favorite styles, all of which are figure flattering and in the one color her future sister-in-law has agreed to wear—purple. Choices are nar-rowed down to two. MOB can't stand purple. Bride isn't wild about it either.

THIRD APPOINTMENT: Bride returns with groom to show him choices for his sister. Groom insists on purple, is ordering purple cummerbunds for all his groomsmen to placate his sister. Groom selects style with long sleeves and an A-line skirt. Writes a check for the fifty percent deposit on sister's dress.

FOURTH APPOINTMENT: Bride returns with MOG to show her the dress selected by groom. MOG worried about SOG (sister of groom), who has been exhibiting increased signs of depression, withdrawal and feelings of being neglected.

FIFTH APPOINTMENT: SOG comes in alone to see dress. No possibility of trying on sample size 12. Bust, waist and hip measurements are estimated amidst grunts and groans and grumblings of, "Why do I have to do this?"

SIXTH APPOINTMENT: Groom returns with bride in tears. SOG doesn't like the dress. Doesn't like the color. Doesn't like the fabric. Doesn't like the price. Perhaps, doesn't like the bride. Bride says she'll start all over.

SEVENTH APPOINTMENT: Bride and MOB return. Find a "tent" style in a darker purple.

EIGHTH APPOINTMENT: Bride and MOG return. MOG suggests to bride that large dark floral bouquets might help to make SOG feel better about herself when she walks down the aisle.

NINTH APPOINTMENT: Groom, perspiring profusely, and SOG arrive. Groom figures that without the bride around, his sister will be more at ease. "Tent" is approved. An inch is added to our previous estimated measurements when SOG announces that she usually gains weight when she's miserable. And she's miserable.

TENTH APPOINTMENT: Three local, livid bridesmaids come in with mutiny on their minds. Why should seven bridesmaids have to wear a purple tent to pacify one boorish bridesmaid? I have no answer to this.

ELEVENTH APPOINTMENT: Groom returns to discuss sizing of SOG's dress with me. Did I measure correctly? No. She wouldn't let me within three feet of her. Would I call her first when dresses arrived so none of the other bridesmaids would be around when she picked up her dress? Sure, I had planned on that anyway. Would I keep news of this appointment from the bride and MOG? He didn't want to be thought of as controlling. No kidding.

NO APPOINTMENT: Father-of-the-groom (FOG) barges in one afternoon in the middle of another bride's appointment, demanding that he see SOG's dress, her measurements, the delivery schedule and photos of other bridesmaids in the dress. Insisting that a half-yard of fabric be ordered to hold up to SOG's face before the order is placed.

TWELFTH APPOINTMENT: Bride comes in by herself to check on the order and select jewelry for her bridesmaids to wear at the wedding.

This was the first time I'd seen her alone. First time in months that she didn't have a keeper with her.

I looked long and hard at this sweet, loving, benevolent, naïve bride....this Stepford-wife-in-training.

I wanted to grab her by her magnanimous little neck, shake her back to some semblance of self-esteem and shout, "RUN...RUN...JUST RUN...DO NOT PASS GO...DO NOT COLLECT $200....JUST RUN...AND NEVER LOOK BACK!!!!"

I didn't.

"You cannot prevent the birds of sorrow from flying over your head, but you can prevent them from building nests in your hair."

Chinese proverb

The Wisdom Of
Louis XVIII

*A*nyone who ever worked with me will tell you that my number one pet peeve was the not-showing-up-at-all/cancelled-at-the-last-minute appointment.

Some bridal shops charge a hefty fee for these no-shows, taking credit card information prior to scheduling the appointment. We never resorted to that, thanks to the kind heart and forgiving nature of Mary Ann, one of our saintly sales associates.

Anyone can be late occasionally. Anyone can forget occasionally. It was the repeat offenders who drew my ire. Mary Ann always offered amnesty, so it was her sorry lot to be the person in charge of calling no-shows.

A typical message left by Mary Ann would go something like this: "We're calling about your one o'clock appointment with us. We were so looking forward to seeing you and your daughter and hope that you weren't in an accident. Hope you're not sick. Hope your daughter isn't sick. Hope your dog isn't sick. Have a nice day."

Sometimes Mrs. I'm-Out-on-the-Golf-Course-and-It's-Too-Nice-a-Day-to-Shop would extend the courtesy of calling us back to say that her neighbor had died and she had been helping the family plan the funeral during the time of her scheduled appointment.

And sometimes Miss I'm-Having-My-Eyebrows-Waxed-and-Look-Too-Puffy-to-Try-on-Wedding-Gowns would bump into me the following day and go into great detail about her miraculous recovery from yesterday's bout of twenty-four-hour stomach flu, a strange illness that had left debilitating puffiness around her eyes.

Mary Ann, a Francophile, loved to quote King Louis XVIII, "Punctuality is the politeness of kings." Wise words from the king who ruled after Napoleon, restoring the Bourbon family to the throne after his brother, Louis XVI, was beheaded.

A punishment I often contemplated for repeat "no-shows."

Thank God for Mary Ann, Chief of Protocol, and Minister of Mercy.

Every bridal boutique should have one.

"Men count up the faults of those who keep them waiting."

Louis XVIII

Chanel Wanna-bes

*C*oco Chanel, born Gabrielle Bonheur Chanel, August 19, 1883, in the town of Saumur, Maine-et-Loire, France, was the second illegitimate daughter of Albert Chanel and Jeanne Devolle.

Abandoned at the age of twelve by a father who ran off after the death of her mother, she became a ward of the state, living until the age of seventeen with nuns in the Aubazine orphanage.

She adapted at an early age, becoming shrewd and pragmatic, and would go on to become, arguably, the most illustrious, most often copied, most widely quoted designer of the twentieth century. She had opinions about anything and everything—and never hesitated to express them.

"Don't spend time beating on a wall, hoping to transform it into a door."

Sisters at the convent in Moulins, her next home, secured a seamstress position for her, a job at which she excelled until boredom and a burning desire to become a cabaret singer consumed her.

Soon she left to begin singing at a café called La Rotonde. Legend has it that it was here that Gabrielle acquired the name Coco, singing what became her trademark song, "*Qui qu'a vu Coco?*" ("Who has seen Coco?") The name stuck. It was here, too, that she discovered men. And men discovered her. Many men.

"As long as you know men are like children, you know everything."

"I never wanted to weigh more heavily on a man than a bird."

Etianne Balson, an English playboy, took her as his mistress and then to Paris, where he convinced her to give up the cabaret life and return to her calling as a seamstress. He financed her first business venture, designing hats.

Her millinery creations were simple and boyish and a far cry from the Belle Epoque chapeaux in style at the time. She designed hats swathed in tulle or chiffon often surrounding wide brims and tying in a large bow under the chin, or smothered in feathers, with ribbons and flora of every kind.

"How can a brain function under those things?"

"Fashion fades, only style remains the same."

Eager to shed the top-heavy, gargantuan bonnets of the time, women flocked to her shop, bringing Coco her first taste of success.

Shortly thereafter, something better came along. Another playboy, Arthur ("Boy") Capel, purportedly the love of her life and with even deeper pockets than Etianne. He backed her expansion, adding boutiques in the coastal resort towns of Biarritz and Deauville to her shop in Paris.

Hats were joined by a full line of clothing designs. She utilized styles, fabrics and articles of clothing such as sports jackets and ties worn by men. Fabrics, often men's fabrics, were soft and fluid and comfortable—a new idea in the still corseted fashion of the day. A loose fitting sweater that she belted and paired with a skirt was one of her first successes.

"Luxury must be comfortable, otherwise it is not luxury."

Meanwhile, she was out and about in Parisian society, spending long hours at the racetrack, climbing the social ladder and refining her look of hidden luxury. She would soon change the way women wanted to dress, literally changing the way they would look at themselves.

"Look for the woman in the dress. If there is no woman, there is no dress."

Then came the "little black dress," and there was no stopping her. Just a nothing of a dress, a blank-slate waiting to be accessorized, worn again and again and again and ultimately immortalized.

"Elegance is refusal."

"Elegance does not consist in putting on a new dress."

In 1923, she introduced the Chanel suit. Shown in several colors, it was a knee-length, boxy-jacketed bit of elegance trimmed in black braid and gold buttons. Large costume pearl necklaces completed the look. A smash combination.

"The best color in the world is the one that looks good on you."

Also, in 1923, as if the "little black dress" and Chanel suit weren't ample successes, she became the first designer to create a perfume bearing her name, Chanel No. 5. Its distinctive scent and classic Art Deco bottle continue, to this day, to make it one of the most sought after, beloved perfumes.

"A woman who doesn't wear perfume has no future."

"One should wear perfume wherever she wants to be kissed."

As her social, professional and sexual progress continued, the name of Coco Chanel was linked with numerous men, some wealthy and persistent suitors. The Duke of Westminster, one of the richest men in Europe, pursued her hand in marriage, to no avail. She refused his proposal.

"There have been several Duchesses of Westminster. There is only one Chanel."

"How many cares one loses when one decides not to be something, but to be someone."

She maintained two apartments in Paris, one at her beloved Ritz Hotel, where she lived, and one above her couture house, at 31 rue Cambon, close to the Ritz, where she entertained. Luxurious Art Deco furniture, sumptuously detailed silver and gold boxes, ornate seventeenth century Chinese wooden screens called coromandels and magnificent crystal chandeliers were beautifully at home within the private celadon walls. An oversized, lengthy couch of the softest tan suede cushioned "Mademoiselle," as she was known, when she entertained those fortunate enough to be invited to her sought-after soirees.

"There is a time for work and a time for love. That leaves no other time."

She had it all.

"A girl should be two things: classy and fabulous."

The scent of Chanel No. 5 wasn't the only thing in the air. War was in the air. Fear was in the air.

New designs and new men continued to dominate her life as World War II broke out in Europe and as the Germans marched into Paris. Soon everything became ugly, including the reputation of Coco Chanel.

It was widely known that she was carrying on an affair with a Nazi officer, Hans Gunther von Dincklage, whose many favors to her included allowing her to continue to live in luxury in her apartment at the Ritz. She closed the door to her business, shutting it down completely.

"Great loves, too, must be endured."

After the war, she was accused of collaborating with the Nazis. When brought in to testify concerning her relationship with von Dinklage, she stated,

"When a woman of sixty encounters a handsome man who wishes to make love to her, she doesn't first inquire as to his politics."

This "disgraced" label stayed with her into her later years, when, in 1954, she decided to re-open the House of Chanel, attempting a comeback.

"A woman has the age she deserves."

"Nature gives you the face you have at twenty; it is up to you to merit the face you have at fifty."

Needless to say her comeback was successful, according her first name recognition and a smash Broadway musical in 1969, starring Katherine Hepburn, entitled simply *Coco*.

She died alone in her private apartment at the Ritz Hotel in Paris at the age of 87, leaving an indelible mark on the world of fashion and redefining the word "style."

"Fashion is not simply a matter of clothes. Fashion is in the air, born upon the wind. One intuits it. It is in the sky and on the road."

Well, dear reader, many an ersatz "Mademoiselle" walked through our door, Chanel wanna-bes, criticizing the neckline of one dress, the bodice of another, positioning a long flowing skirt over a short tight skirt, announcing to all within earshot that this was the way the designer should have constructed that dress.

Never was this taken to greater lengths than at Cheryl Jackson's spring wedding, held in her aunt's Kansas City showcase garden. Lilac bridesmaid dresses with an organza overlay covering the floor length skirt and softening the strapless top with a cap-sleeved bolero had been chosen by the bride for her eleven attendants.

Her dream, her vision, was to capture herself, the bride, surrounded by her bridesmaids, an early evening pale blue spring sky above and her aunt's prize-winning lilac bushes framing them all in a full color photograph.

As luck would have it, Mother Nature shone down upon the blossoming-on-schedule lilac bushes, the glorious spring day and the radiant bridal party. The photographer captured the bride's dream and, to this day, the pastel photo is proudly displayed in her home.

Ten minutes after capturing this vision, one of her bridesmaids, brandishing long, orange-handled scissors, proceeded to chop, chop off her lilac organza floor length skirt creating a raggedy-above-the-knee length, proclaiming it to be a much more stylish look. Next on her attack, were the cap sleeves, butchered to sleeveless status. According to her, a much trendier look.

Yes, aghast reader, this really happened. Amazingly, bride and the Chanel wanna-be remain good friends, attesting to the expansiveness of the friendships of women.

"There goes a woman who knows all the things
that can be taught and none of the things
that can't be taught."

Coco Chanel

Dow And Jones

One of the most frequent questions I would be asked concerned the correct length of skirts to wear and when to wear them:

Floor length before 5:00 p.m?

Floor length after 5:00 p.m?

Tea length? (And what the hell is T-length?)

Ankle length?

Maxi? Then, how do I walk?

Mini? Then, how do I sit?

Mr. Dow and Mr. Jones, who presumably had a Mrs. Dow and Mrs. Jones, have often had something to say about this age-old dilemma. Controversy continues as to whether the stock market drives the fashion industry or vice versa. Who knows if this chicken-before-the-egg riddle will ever be solved, but we do know that during the roaring twenties stocks were going crazy at an all time high, and so were the flappers' dresses. Until the crash came in 1929, and both stocks and hemlines plummeted.

Twiggy burst upon the scene in the 1960s, with stick-skinny legs and skirts up to her—well, they were up pretty high. As was the stock market. Mini-skirts and the New York Stock Exchange were in perfect harmony.

And then, dear fashion savvy reader, remember the maxi-skirts of the early 1970s? Down to our trim ankles they fell, along with supplies of gasoline caused by the Arab oil embargo. We stood in long lines at the gas pumps, our knees, calves and ankles toasty warm throughout that cruel winter in our long maxis.

After hitting a record 14,000 shares in the summer of 2007, with short skirts everywhere, 7th Avenue is predicting lower hemlines for the spring of 2008. Bad news? Who knows, but, dear financially savvy reader, I'd take a hard look at my portfolio first, my wardrobe second.

Would that questions from brides, mother and bridesmaids could be as easily answered as stock market buy or sell queries. Here again, my standard advice would apply: accentuate the positive, eliminate the negative.

- If you have piano-leg legs, go floor length from 10:00 a.m. to midnight.
- If you have ham hock knees like me, try ending your skirt just below the knee.
- If you have Mary Hart knees (pray to God, not her voice), hike that skirt up above those shapely gams and flaunt them.
- And never, never, ever wear a skirt that hits the middle of your calf, unless you want to complete the ensemble with dowdy pumps, a little round purse containing nothing, white gloves, a double strand of pearls and a blue cloche hat in imitation of an eighty-year-old Queen Elizabeth, one incredible lady, in spite of her majestic frowziness.

Such to-do over such inconsequence!

*"I believe that all wisdom consists in caring
immensely for a few right things,
and not caring a straw about the rest."*

John Buchan

All's Well That Ends Well

𝒩ot a week would pass by without someone asking me to keep a secret. For the most part, happy secrets.

"I just found out I'm pregnant, Mrs. Crowell, and haven't even told my husband yet. I'm calling to ask you to order my bridesmaid dress for Janet's wedding in a size 14 instead of a size 10."

"I'm calling to schedule an appointment to look at wedding gowns. Michael and I are going to Hawaii next week, and I just know he's going to propose to me. But I don't want anyone to see me trying on dresses. Can you schedule me in at an odd time?"

"My sister just got engaged, but she hasn't told our mother yet. If we come in to look at dresses, please don't say anything to my mother if you bump into her at the grocery store."

"We're calling off the wedding. Irreconcilable differences before we even get started. Cindy's coming to pick up her bridesmaid dress tomorrow. Don't say anything to her."

"I just got my ring last night. I'm so excited I can hardly stand it, but we're not telling anyone until my dad gets back in town next week. Can I come in tomorrow and try on wedding gowns? Sometime when no one I know will be in the shop?"

Well, this one didn't work out as planned.

Freshly engaged young lady arrives as scheduled at 2:30. Saintly sales associate and I duly exclaim over her pro-offered sparkling left hand. Ecstatic bride-to-be tries on three wedding gowns. As the fourth creation is being brought into the dressing room, freshly engaged, bride-to-be's future mother-in-law waltzes into the store. Unannounced. No appointment. Just picking up her daughter's dress for the upcoming holiday debutante ball.

"My daughter and I are about the same size," says she. "I think I'll pop into the dressing room and try her dress on."

Saintly sales associate goes apoplectic. Whisks ecstatic bride-to-be, half-clad in a beaded white satin gown, out of adjoining dressing room containing her clueless mother-in-law-to-be and catapults her into the stock room, sandwiching her in between two large racks of long gowns. Bride-to-be in a panic. "Not to worry," soothes saintly sales associate. "Little chance of her coming in here."

Phone rings. Saintly sales associate answers the phone, busily scheduling an appointment. Clueless mother-in-law-to-be realizes that she doesn't have a gown for herself to wear to the debutante ball. Marches into the stock room, looking through the gowns hanging from the size 8 rack and finds a dumbstruck, very familiar face smashed between the size 6s and 10s. Her son's girlfriend, all color drained from her face, half covered in white satin, not knowing whether to laugh or cry.

Wisely, saintly sales associate and I disappear.

So much for subterfuge.

Fortunately, hugs and kisses and tears are exchanged and shed—and, as The Bard so distinctively would say, all was well that ended well.

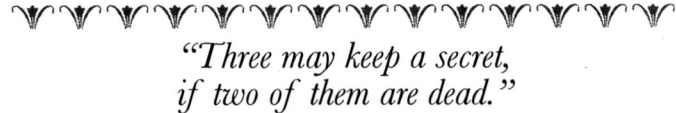

"Three may keep a secret,
if two of them are dead."

Benjamin Franklin

*A Girl With Spunk—
and I Like Spunk*

*E*ighteen-year-old college freshmen, especially convent schooled young ladies, many from my alma-mater, keen on being unregimented and freewheeling for the first time in their young lives, were some of my favorite clients.

Emily O'Malley, the youngest of five sisters, was finally getting her turn to test her independence at Northwestern University, returning home at Christmas for the annual debutante ball, a benefit event raising over two million dollars for Cardinal Glennon Children's Hospital in St. Louis. All four older sisters had walked the walk, curtsied to the Archbishop and danced the first dance to the strains of "Thank Heaven for Little Girls" with their proud, thinner-walleted father.

Emily knew the routine well. Knew the rules and regulations.

- All white, long, full-skirted gown.
- Long, white leather gloves.
- Minimum, tasteful jewelry.
- Closed toe, white fabric, one-and-a-half inch high pumps.
- Full crinoline petticoat under skirt so spotlights don't create see-through look.
- No strapless gown.
- No low cut gown that would necessitate a generous piece of white fabric being inserted to conceal décolletage.

One of the last debutantes to be presented by their fathers, Miss Emily Whitworth O'Malley was announced to the one thousand plus guests assembled at lavishly decorated tables in the candlelit ballroom. On the right arm of her father, holding a large bouquet of pale pink roses in her left arm, she entered the ballroom, stepping daintily onto the pristine, white, elevated runway, her auburn curls sparkling under the bright spotlights, Irish eyes twinkling with excitement, in anticipation of the long white runway stretching in front of her. Begowned and tuxedoed friends, family and strangers, their eyes fixed solely on her, greeted her as she made her way down the runway, slowly, step by careful step. Honoring the traditional debutante walk: left foot forward, right foot meeting left foot; right foot forward, left foot meeting right foot; and so on.

To her left, she spied her mother and four sisters seated at their table right next to the runway, beaming as their daughter/sister approached them.

Four left-foot steps away from their table, Emily's eyes signaled, "Watch this." Her left hand holding her bouquet moved slowly down to the left side of her gown, and one left-foot step before reaching the family table, she hiked her white taffeta gown up approximately ten inches to reveal flaming red cowboy boots—much to her mother's horror and her sisters' delight.

Oh, how I miss those indomitable, and, yes, spunky eighteen-year-old Emilys.

"When in doubt, wear red."

Bill Blass

A Male Perspective

*O*ccasionally, an actual man would walk through our door.

Men intent on their wives or girlfriends selecting a dress to highlight their various assets...(i.e., boobs).

Men intent on their wives or girlfriends selecting a dress to conceal their various assets...(i.e., boobs).

Men wanting to take a peak at a beloved daughter in her wedding gown, to steel himself for the real thing when he would walk her down the aisle.

Men who controlled the purse strings, strolling in to sign on the dotted line.

Men with nothing to do on a Saturday afternoon, just wanting to ogle a bunch of pretty girls parading by in strapless dresses.

Men dragged in by nagging wives, who eventually would disappear into my office where a strategically placed armchair and TV set tuned into Notre Dame and/or Mizzou football games were in wait. (Cardinal games for summer appointments.)

One man, a cross-dresser, who just loved our long gowns, mercifully placed only one special order, re-quiring only one cautious trip into the dressing room to take his measurements.

Men wanting their wives to look drop-dead gor-geous on various special occasions, coming in with opinions, compliments and an open wallet.

One such man, with a lovely petite wife and three beautiful daughters, was a regular. His philosophy: my wife and daughters look at themselves just once in the mirror before they go out and I, happily, look at them for the entire evening.

So, for every big event in their lives, the wife and daughters would schedule several appointments to select their favorite gowns and accessories, bringing Dad in at the very end for final approval.

Not for everyone, but it worked for them.

*"I think men who have a pierced ear
are better prepared for marriage.
They've experienced pain and bought jewelry."*

Rita Rudner

Mayday, Mayday

St. Louis is a city that holds tight to tradition. Dancing the Maypole is one such tradition.

Every May, weather permitting, young ladies in long white gowns, students at two private high schools in St. Louis, dance around a tall pole secured at the top with multi-colored ribbons. It is a custom and a symbolism steeped with ancient history in celebration of pagan fertility, an irony not lost on many a chaste senior, poised to master her first Maypole steps.

Hours of practice are required to perfect this graceful, complicated dance, each girl holding a long four-inch wide colored streamer, weaving and dancing in and out of a circular pattern. All this around a ten-foot high pole, intertwining ribbons on the pole and creating a colorful plaited web at the conclusion of the dance.

Sounds easy? I assure you, dear reader, it is not.

My initiation to this ancient rite, along with my twenty-eight other classmates, came in 1955 at the hands of our gym teacher, a sturdy, hatchet-nosed, take-no-prisoners drill sergeant spinster from North Dakota. She was as butch as it gets, lived on the school grounds with her Irish Setter, Pat, and was simultaneously feared and loved by all. As far as we were concerned, she was grounds keeper, Phys. Ed. teacher, school nurse, counselor, after-school tutor, coach, principal and friend. She ran the place.

Gym class slackers still shudder, recalling the whack she would give them with the flat end of her field hockey stick, smacking their rear ends while they ran as fast as they could down a hilly forest path—down the twisting narrow, often slippery, wooded path and over the wide rushing brook below, navigating the moss-covered, slimy rocks, gingerly step-stoning across to the hockey field beyond. All this with gym teacher's terrifying hockey stick and loveable, featherbrained Irish Setter flailing behind.

For thirty years, she commandeered unbeatable field hockey and basketball teams, instilling fear in every opposing team. Forced retirement came only when she could no longer hurl herself and her hockey stick down the treacherous path to the hockey field. She did not go gently into the night.

On a lovely spring day, after enduring endless hours of practice with her in command, I donned my long, white organza gown and pale blue sash, designating the color of my streamer. Along with the rest of my class, I marched down the slippery, grassy knoll onto the freshly mowed bowl at my convent school and surveyed the enormous crowd of family and friends awaiting the beginning of this annual spring rite. Forming a perfect circle with my classmates around the Maypole, I picked up the end of my pale blue streamer resting on the grass, listened for the first strains of "Waltz of the Wood Nymphs," and, with spirits soaring, nerves multiplying and counts of "one, two, three, under the pink, one, two, three over the yellow" pounding in my head, we all began.

Dear Jynn—
Hope you'll
enjoy this silly
little book and
will feel your friends
about it.

Judy

"A Shop's Fables"

Charmingly, at first.

We danced. We floated. We pirouetted and waltzed. We went under streamers. In and out of streamers. Over streamers. The top of the Maypole became resplendent with at least twelve inches of perfectly braided pink, yellow, blue, lavender and green ribbons.

Mothers beamed, making sure that everyone in their vicinity knew which virginal darling belonged to them. Fathers whistled and cheered. Little sisters, poised on the very edge of their wooden folding chairs, couldn't wait for their turn at this hallowed tradition. Brothers yawned, praying for a screw-up. Which didn't take long.

Mary Alice zigged when she should have zagged. And things went downhill from there.

A "pink sash" tripped on the hem of a "yellow," throwing all the "one, two, three" counts out of sync and causing a chain reaction, a perfect circle, of muffled, uncontrolled giggles. Tangles and one-colored contorted knots were forming on the pole. Two girls dropped their streamers and bumped heads bending down, in very unladylike fashion, to retrieve them.

Sidney Squirrel, perched precariously on a high branch of a one hundred and twenty-year-old oak tree at the edge of the bowl, spied Sally Squirrel, resting prettily on a nearby branch, and, inspired by the bouquet of spring in the air and the merriment of the pagan fertility rite unfolding through the branches of leafy-tipped leaves below him, determined to make her his own. Around and around the jagged bark of the oak tree he pursued her. In dizzying circles he arrived inches behind her at the bottom of the tree, heading lickety-split for the center of the Maypole dance, then in frenzied progress.

Not to miss out on a chance of squirrel stew, Pat, the rambunctious Irish Setter, bolted from his mistress's side, knocking over a "green sash" as he entered the circle in hot pursuit of Sidney and Sally who were falling in love at the base of the pole.

It was a pastel disaster.

Somehow or another, we rallied, passing along whispered encouragements and hurrahs to each other, trying to salvage at least a modicum of class pride.

At the completion of the dance, mothers were no longer pointing out their virginal darlings to strangers seated next to them, fathers were questioning years of writing tuition checks, little sisters were snickering, smug in the realization that they'd get it right when their turns came, and brothers were wide awake, hootin' and hollerin' and loving every goofy, Laurel and Hardy minute of the fiasco.

At the conclusion of the dance, the top third of the pole was evenly, artistically plaited to perfection, the center a muddled, jumbled, holy mess and the bottom third a re-creation of botched weaving similar to what we had achieved in our first practice session. At least, we had completed it.

The Maypole of 1955 would go down in the annals of school history as May mayhem, prefaced with, "Remember the year that..."

Looking back on it, with the rose-colored perspective of fifty years, I wouldn't change a thing. It was one helluva performance.

A few days after our dance debacle, our long white dresses were to be worn again for graduation. Mercifully, no streamers, Irish setters or squirrels involved in this ritual.

Years later my daughter, Lisa—my baby—would repeat these two rituals with many more classmates than I'd had and much less trauma. Our shared alma mater was one of five schools in the area requiring seniors to wear long white dresses for graduation.

I couldn't believe my last child, my baby, was graduating. Hadn't it been just yesterday that I had walked her into kindergarten? And where was I going to find a long white dress for her? Something full-skirted, simple, with just the right amount of embellishment on it and in keeping with the school requirements.

My class of 1955, all twenty-nine of us, had voted on and worn the same dress. I still can't figure out how we ever pulled that off. It was a white organza gown with a very full skirt, short sleeves, a high, really high neck, Peter Pan collar, self-fabric belt and tiny pearl buttons down the front of the bodice. The epitome of modesty. The essence of chastity. How things had changed.

I discovered that many mothers had already hired seamstresses to make their daughters' dresses. A few had shopped in Chicago and New York, and a few had bedraggled hand-me-downs from older sisters.

Aha, said I. *Now that I have my new retail space in Ladue, why don't I bring a collection of long white dresses into the store? Test the waters. What do I have to lose? I'll at least get a beautiful dress for my daughter out of it.*

Prior to taking a large suite of rooms in the building behind and conducting business by appointment only, I had rented an open, airy retail space with three walls of floor-to-ceiling windows and a loft area on the second floor, reached by courageously ascending a narrow, black wrought iron spiral staircase. Think firehouse. Not the most practical arrangement, since every single enormous box filled with gowns had to be wriggled up the staircase, gowns steamed to perfection and then painstakingly brought back down the stairs to hang on display racks in the showroom.

I made a quick trip to 7th Avenue, resulting in a respectable selection of dresses. We sent out some flyers, put an ad in the local paper and hoped for a few shoppers to come by for the trunk show, scheduled for the last Saturday and Sunday of January, from 10:00 a.m. to 5:00 p.m..

My sales staff stayed late with me Friday night, displaying the collection in the center room, preparing for Saturday morning store opening at ten. I had asked them to report in at eight-thirty on Saturday to straighten up the loft area and make any last minute preparations. All of which were completed before nine, when I left for some coffee and a breather upstairs for all of us before store hours began.

At 9:20, while relaxing, sipping our coffee and chatting, we heard voices outside. A bit of a commotion. Our loft had a skylight, but no windows, so I went to the top of the spiral stairs to bend over and see what was going on outside.

Oh, my God.

At least two hundred mothers and daughters were pressed against all three outside glass walls, pushing and shoving, frozen noses and hands smashed against the windows, clawing to get in, vying for pole position in an attempt to be one of the first to barge through our one standard size front door.

Mayday! Mayday!

We had a hatchway on the back wall of the loft, leading out to the roof, an escape route required by code, and every time we would peek down at the mushrooming crowd, we wanted to bolt through the hatchway and hide on the roof until 5:00 p.m. Sunday.

At 9:59, not a moment sooner, my two saleswomen and I made our way down the spiral staircase, inhaled deep breaths, wished each other luck and, with great trepidation, opened the front door.

Bedlam.

For eight hours, we passed long white dresses over the heads of customers, back and forth to triumphant souls who had conquered the dressing rooms. At the end of this brutal ninety-six hour weekend, I bestowed blessings (and a raise) on my saleswomen, designating them "saintly sales associates" for the first time, bypassing the beatification process entirely and elevating them to sainthood without further ado.

We had certainly found a niche, and in following years perfected The Graduation Gown Collection, extending the time frame to three weeks in January and the hours from 10:00 a.m. to 9:00 p.m., and making it one of the most anticipated, enjoyable events of the year.

Invitations were sent to seniors at all five schools. Leisurely appointments of one-and-a-half hours allowed each mother and graduate our undivided attention and assistance. Every year we made good on our promise not to sell the same gown to more than one girl at each school, thereby insuring that no two graduates would appear wearing the same dress.

Pressure to secure one of the first appointment slots became so great that we were forced to begin a set-in-stone date and time, 10:00 a.m., when we would begin accepting phone calls and scheduling appointments. With my two saintly sales associates, the ones who had survived The Graduation Collection #1, I barricaded myself in the store office, blinds closed, lights out, hands poised to answer the phone. Two of us took calls, one of us frantically scheduling appointments on the graph we had designed, making sure not to double book the hour-and-a-half slots. We looked liked a Ticketmaster office selling seats for an Elton John concert.

Creative tactics were employed to get the earliest time slots. A few mothers came in person, banging on our locked door, hoping to interrupt us during the incessant ringing of the phones. Calls came in months, weeks, days in advance of the 10:00 a.m. start time: "I'll be out of town"; "I'll be at my mother's bedside"; "I'll be at my mother's funeral"; "My daughter got an A on her report card and I promised her I'd get her one of the first appointments"; "I'm not feeling well and will probably be sick then"; etc., etc., etc.

We were steadfast—no, draconian—in keeping to the 10:00 a.m. start time, unwavering in this orderly method of being fair to all. Seen, perhaps, as cantankerous by some. But then, they hadn't been around for the first one.

Over the years, we sold over two thousand long white gowns for graduation, all within the strict guidelines of each school. A Berrybridge gown became as much a part of graduation as commencement speeches, the awarding of diplomas and tossing of mortarboards.

Janell Berte, well-known designer of debutante and wedding gowns, understood exactly what these young women were looking for. From the age of twelve, she was smitten with design, eventually working at Giorgio's on Rodeo Drive in Beverly Hills, designing for celebrities including Fay Wray, Jill Ireland and Zsa Zsa Gabor. Soon her clothes were available at I. Magnin, Neiman Marcus and Saks Fifth Avenue. Weary of smog, mudslides and earthquakes, Berte moved her business to the heart of Amish country in Lancaster, Pennsylvania, where she continues to be sought after by discriminating brides.

For several years, my sales associates and I would come up with new styles for the graduates, wondering every year if we could keep creating new and exciting designs within the confines of the schools' restrictions. Many a night I'd go to bed counting white dresses instead of sheep.

It was the most exhausting three weeks of the year. I loved it and still miss these young women. So full of expectation and so eager to graduate, to stretch their wings and head far away from home to college life. Excitement tempered with the sadness of leaving classmates and home. Bittersweet emotions for them and for their mothers, as one phase of life ended and another began.

These emotions gave rise to our own little Berrybridge tradition of Kleenex boxes stashed in strategic places throughout the store. One more St. Louis tradition.

"How did it get late so soon?
It's night before it's noon.
December is here before it's June. My goodness how
the time has flewn.
How did it get late so soon?"

Dr. Seuss

W.W.M.D.
(What Would Martha Do)

*D*o you have any idea, dear reader, of how much a stack of thirty-three bridal magazines weighs? Can you even begin to imagine how injurious it is to a betrothed maiden's nubile spinal column to lift a twenty-one-pound stack of glossy, wish-upon-a-star, dream-sheets out of the back seat of a BMW 328i, stagger across the parking lot in hopes of finding a sympathetic doorman positioned at the entry to the bridal boutique, and, with a resounding thud, drop the entire load onto the nearest tabletop? Do you have the slightest idea of the ensuing anxiety and angst this action can cause to a long-suffering bridal boutique owner?

I do.

What follows is as predictable as an older sister's unsolicited advice.

Fluttering madly away at the edges of each magazine will be at least twenty little yellow Post-Its, each one indicating a longed-for neckline, fabric, trim, beadwork, etc., etc., etc. Blushing betrothed will reverently lift the latest spring issue from the top of the stack, making certain at all times that the fourth finger of her left hand is in sparkle position, as one by one she pours through the Post-Its, oohing and aahing over each perfect neckline, each to-die-for billowing skirt, each beyond-compare beading.

Whereupon long-suffering bridal boutique owner will reach a semi-catatonic state. Her eyes will glaze over as she calls upon every last reserve of composure to tactfully suggest, "They all have lovely features. I'm sure that if all these features were put together, they would create a beautiful gown. We have equally beautiful gowns to show you. So, why don't we begin with some of our top designers?"

And a dose of reality.

Out of this towering stack of thirty-three glossies, nine times out of ten, at least twenty or more are from Martha. Martha Stewart Weddings. Martha Stewart Living. Martha Stewart Everyday Food. Martha Stewart Body + Soul. Martha Stewart How-To-Get-Up-In-The-Morning. Martha Stewart How-To-Go-To-Bed-At-Night.

Martha had wedding reception advice ranging from French patisserie-style sponge cakes with chocolate calligraphy monograms to pomegranate champagne cocktails. She knew how to coordinate a soft pink roses bridal bouquet with soft pink roses blusher and foundation. How to create an eyelet themed wedding awash in eyelet trimmed napkins, place cards, pillows, favors, corsages and, of course, wedding gowns.

An interesting concept, this advice thing. Some live by the old maxim that the best advice is to neither give it or take it. Certainly not Martha.

Along with all the other solicited and unsolicited advice given out under our roof, Martha was never out of the loop—not even during her sojourn in the Big

House. What would Martha do was and continues to be an ongoing refrain.

"Advice is what we ask for when we already know the answer, but wish we didn't."

Erica Jong

Bridal Shopper's Ten Commandments

1. Thou shalt leave thy pre-pubescent children with their battery-operated toys and M&Ms at home.

2. Thou shalt not wear red lace bras or purple thongs to try on white gowns. Bottom line: thou shalt wear underwear.

3. Thou shalt not, on seeing price tag of bridal gown, exclaim, "Good God, I could cover my monthly mortgage, make a car payment, buy a new dishwasher and still have enough money left for a Starbucks venti dolce latte for the price of that dress!"

4. Thou shalt not covet thy best friend's color scheme, bridesmaid dresses, floral arrangements or fiancé.

5. Thou shalt not attempt to squeeze thy size 22 hips into size 10 samples.

6. Thou shalt honor thy mother's unrealistic expectations and thy father's credit card limits.

7. Thou shalt not harass, demean or annoy saintly sales associates unless they call thou "honey" five times or more.

8. Thou shalt not take the name of thy future mother-in-law in vain.

9. Thou shalt not try on a dozen or more Vera Wang couture $12,000 gowns if thy budget is $650.

10. Thou shalt not leave piles of lilac, mint-green, periwinkle, fuschia and taupe bridesmaid dresses in a psychedelic heap on the dressing room floor to be picked up by thy saintly sales associates.

Lacey

I have a granddaughter of marriageable age. Her name is Lacey. She is twenty-five years old, five foot, twelve inches tall in suntanned bare feet, blonde, willowy and drop-dead gorgeous.

When she's ready to walk down the aisle, I hope to be able to sign off on the lucky guy, be invited along for the dress search, and manage to keep my mouth shut.

Probably won't be the opportune time to reminisce about brides of the 1950s (moi) and expound on the twenty-first century version.

Fifty years ago, Priscilla of Boston was the most sought after designer of wedding gowns (my designer of choice), and as I gaze upon the downcast eyes, blonde pageboy hairstyle, single strand of pearls, Spanish mantilla lace veil and demure profile of the black and white formal wedding photograph, sunlit by the evening sunset and hanging on my living room wall, I realize that my gown could very well be part of the inventory of any current upscale bridal boutique. Easily worn with style by a bride of today.

Maybe Lacey?

Following the wild, non-conformist days of the roaring twenties, when brides were married in black velvet, underwater and atop flagpoles, the 1950s ushered in a period of more formal, elaborate wedding traditions.

"Something old, something new, something borrowed, something blue" returned along with the emotional strains of "O Promise Me" and Wagner's "Lohengrin." Bridal bouquets of lilies of the valley, white roses and freesia were tossed to virginal, hearts-a-pounding, petal-pink clad bridesmaids, who would instantly turn into Green Bay Packer linesmen when it was time for the bride to toss the bouquet, throwing a block onto opposing petal-pink clad hopefuls going out for the ten-yard pass—a completion that would guarantee being next in line to wed.

I married in an age of great affluence. Hard to believe now, when, at the time, the average annual income was $3,200, the cost of a house approximately $10,000, and a top-of-the-line, pure silk and lace designer wedding gown around $350.

Grace Kelly, in a long sleeved, high-necked lace confection, wed her prince, bringing modesty, high fashion and unrealistic marital expectations back into vogue.

Black and white television entertained us with families and marriages of domestic perfection. Brides cooked and cleaned and cleaned and cooked, all in pearls and high heels. Mothers kept their twenty-three-inch waists and belted hourglass figures intact, their hair coiffed, and their 2.3 children in tow with a perky nod of their heads and occasional scowl. Larger disciplinary problems awaited the return home of the gray-flannel-suited husband, following a day at the office climbing the corporate ladder, a husband and father who always knew best. Resolving all problems in a tidy one-half hour, interrupted only by a smooth talking doctor promoting Lucky Strike cigarettes and a classy blonde Betty Furness extolling the virtues of Westinghouse refrigerators.

We liked Ike and Elvis and pink Cadillac convertibles with tailfins.

"Wives should always be lovers, too," warned Burt Bacharach. Just because we had a ring on our finger didn't mean we could greet our man in the gray flannel suit at the door with anything less than freshly applied make-up, his beaming 2.3 children and creamy tuna casseroles in the oven.

We landed our man in the last generation of innocence, when sock-hops, malt shops and movie drive-ins (well, maybe not those) were the parent-sanctioned, Good Housekeeping Seal of Approval venues of courtship.

Young ladies never, never, never called a boy. You went to the dance with Chad. Danced with Troy, Bobby, Ray, T.R., Jack, Bert and Tab. And always, always, always came home with Chad.

We excelled in flirting, necking, petting and parking. Each activity defined in inches by clear-cut anatomical boundaries above or below the neck or waist. When these boundaries were surrendered, ambushed or assaulted, sixty percent resulted in either "shotgun" marriages or impromptu, nine month, cross country visits to Aunt Virginia's.

The credit card and The Pill were invented. Girls went to high school to go steady, to junior colleges to get pinned and to college to get married.

In Korea, a police action, later properly designated a war, raged on. Unlike Vietnam, it didn't come into our living rooms, so we lingered for a while with Ozzie and Harriett, emulated Donna Reed a bit longer and took little notice of the 38th Parallel a world away. We were oblivious to the lurking menaces of the Cold War, bomb shelters and Richard Nixon.

This was my world when I said "I do" in my Priscilla of Boston white silk gown.

My granddaughter's world has been and will be much different when she utters her own "I do." And yet, and yet….

As far as I know, fathers, filled with anticipation and pride, still walk their daughters down the aisle. Grooms still hold back tears when their brides, lovely in silk and white and pearls, first come into view. Mothers still stifle sobs and weep into lace-edged hankies as their children pledge themselves to another. Hands are still held. Hearts still connect and promises continue to be made.

Flirting still happens. It's called on-line dating.

Necking occurs. It's called foreplay. Petting has become shagging and parking has moved to the bedroom. Or office supply room. Kitchen table. Or elevator.

Philosophers, historians, trash journalists, moralists, religious leaders, women libbers and conservative pundits have written volumes on these changing traditions and sexual mores.

I'm not about to go there.

The Phyllis Schlaflys, Betty Friedans and Dear Abbys of this world have all had their say on these matters, but for my money, the wisest commentary on the entire phenomenon comes from a short, stout, white tuxedo-clad piano player in an exotic gin joint in Casablanca. Another guy named Sam.

Moonlight and love songs, never out of date,
Hearts full of gladness, jealousy and hate,
Woman needs man and man must have his mate,
On that you can rely.
The fundamental things apply
As time goes by.
Amen.

So, my Lacey, my lovely granddaughter of the twenty-first century, will go on to love and learn and to one day come to me and ask for my help in finding the perfect wedding gown. Along with my daughter, her mother, we'll set off on this frivolous rite of passage, armed with the Ten Commandments for Bridal Shoppers, probably breaking half of them and disregarding every piece of advice I've ever given within the first half-hour.

What I do hope for, as I have hoped for all my brides, is that she will remember her wedding day clearly and with a full heart for the rest of her life. Remembering it as the beginning it was. Not as an end result of months of shopping and planning.

It takes a long time to become young enough, brave enough to remember again. To remember the love and courage of a walk down the aisle. A nervous groom and a life of unknowns waiting at the end of that walk.

Can there be anything more challenging? More intoxicating? More terrifying?

When that kind of love comes along, the kind that makes you want to walk down that aisle, grab on and never let go.

I did. Once.

It ended with "death do us part."

I yearn for more.

More fundamental things.

Less frivolous things.

But I digress.

Another time, another story.

Perhaps.

Acknowledgements

Ever since Gutenberg's invention of the printing press, authors have used the acknowledgement pages to lavish praise and gratitude upon their agents and editors. That won't happen here.

In this Catch-22 age of publishing, when publishers won't talk to you unless you have an agent, and agents won't talk to you unless you've been published, what's a girl to do?

After accumulating enough rejection slips to wallpaper two bedrooms and a powder room, this girl found her own "editors," her own first readers to whom she will be forever indebted: Carolyn Bower, neighbor and punctuationist extraordinaire; Charles Constantin, my too-far-away-in-San-Francisco muse; Cork Millner, Santa Barbara Writers Conference workshop leader and author of *Portraits, Hollywood Be Thy Name* and *Write from the Start*; Sanny Moore, saintly sales associate; Kathleen Munsch, walking, listening friend of wisdom; everyone at BookSurge, for eliminating much of the angst involved in a first time publishing experience; Paul Munsch, charming FOB and FOG with valued perspective; Mary Ann O'Neill, Chief of Protocol and Minister of Mercy; Nancy Pollnow, friend of fifty plus years; Caryl Simon, adventurous friend of encouraging and constructive criticism; Lynn Beall, Alicia Elsner, Annie Lazarus and Rebecca Rahm, all wonderful friends and movers and shakers at KSDK-TV, an NBC affiliate in St. Louis, frequently the number one station in the country; and Gina Winkler, twenty-something fashionista and computer angel.

Special thanks to my own "agents" and "PR" teams who hosted book-club events from Lake Forest to Palm Beach and Nantucket to Santa Barbara. Events overflowing with Starbucks decaf, Crispy-Crème donuts, Pinot Noir, camembert cheeses and enough tales of their own special-occasion mishaps to launch a sequel to this book.

Thanks to Bob Fanter for his artistry and patience and for being able to envision a peacock in white-tie and tails, a swan swathed in tulle, and a golden retriever as owner of a bridal boutique.

Next usually come the flowery thank-yous to long-suffering family members. Lucky me. I have the best family members—and no suffering to report.

To my daughter, Kim, the real fashion maven, thanks for pounding the pavement of 7th Avenue with me, turning many a working buying trip into a vacation. Thanks, too, for handling things when we were contacted by various media and for furnishing countless quotes on the "latest styles." Keeping up with all the "latest styles" has always been low on my list of priorities, so I'm also grateful for all the times Kim kept a straight face when I was cornered by magazine and newspaper fashion editors and daytime television producers. Pressured into replying and being quoted on all those nonsensical trends and "latest styles"—which height heel to wear with which length dress, which colors were "in," which colors were "out." Spare me!

Thanks to my son-on-law, Andy, who was supportive of the process of writing this book, clueless about the subject matter, and, I know, will one day make a dashing and extremely proud SFOB (step-father of the bride) when my granddaughter, Lacey, walks down the aisle.

Special thanks to my daughter, Lisa, who probably *has* suffered through this project. As my 24/7 computer support system, she would just roll her eyes, heave a deep sigh, and say, "Mom, you sure are pretty" as the 3,745th stupid computer question came her way. A whirlwind trip to Paris, resulting in the discovery of avant-garde designer, Max Chaoul, helped to ease some of this computer generated suffering. Merci beaucoup, Lisa.

Thanks to Lacey, for just being Lacey, and to my grandsons, Andy, Jr., Will and Nick, for furnishing hugs and comic relief when sorely needed.

Thanks to the Ermas, Benjamins, Ericas, Oscars and Mr. or Ms. Anonymous for quotes and words wiser and wittier than mine.

Special thanks to Edgar, whose following inspirational quotation got me through many a morning with pen in hand, staring at a blank piece of loose-leaf paper. An innocent little eight-by-ten piece of paper that with each passing unproductive minute would loom larger and larger in my head, until it was the size of a garage door.

"He started to sing as he tackled the thing
That couldn't be done,
And he did it."
Edgar A. Guest

Last but not least, kudos to that fine, old fellow, Aesop, whose delightful morality tales inspired not only this text, but the charming illustrations by Bob Fanter. What little is known about Aesop: He was born of African origin in 620 BC and lived most of his life as a slave and story-teller in ancient Greece. At some point in later life, he was freed from slavery, dying a violent death around 560 BC in Delphi and leaving behind a treasury of simple, captivating allegories that have been lovingly read to generations and generations of sleepy-headed children at bedtime.

Thanks, Aesop. I'll bet you never thought you'd end up in a silly little book of anecdotes about brides, bangles, beads and brouhahas.

About the Author

Judith (Judy) Crowell is a freelance writer and Travel Editor for St. Louis Seasons Magazine. A mother and grandmother, she currently divides her time between St. Louis, Missouri and Santa Barbara, California.

She can be visited at her website **www.judithcrowell.com.**